*He'd never done anything like this, had never thought for a moment that the evening would lead him here, to Fran's bed.*

Never in his wildest imaginings had he dreamed of anything as spectacularly all-consuming or earthy as their frenzied coupling. He'd never behaved like that in his life, never needed a woman as he had needed Fran tonight.

She moved against him, slowly waking, then lifted her head and looked down at him and smiled.

"Hi," she said, and softly kissed him.

He felt tenderness well up inside him, tenderness and regret, and wished they could have a future together.

"Are you all right?" he asked her softly, and she nodded.

"I'm fine. You?"

"I'm fine," he lied, but he wasn't. He wished with all his heart that he could turn the clock back.

*Double Destiny*

### The right man for Fran?

When nurse Fran Williams reaches a turning point
in her life she finds herself being offered work assignments
with two very different men—men who will offer Fran
more than a job! She doesn't know it, but they
represent her future happiness.

### So which is the right man for Fran?

Is it rich, wealthy, energetic Josh Nicholson,
injured, impatient but gorgeous hero number one?
Or is it charming, sensual, tender Dr. Xavier Giraud,
the single father who needs a woman
to love him and his children?

### Or is there more than one Mr. Right?

Find out and explore Fran's parallel lives
with each of these heroes in
*Assignment: Single Man* (December 2002) and
*Assignment: Single Father* from Harlequin Romance®.

### DOUBLE DESTINY

There is more than one route to happiness

Like to see Fran's introduction
to Josh Nicholson and Xavier Giraud?
Caroline Anderson's prequel
to this intriguing duet is available online.
Look for *Double Destiny* at www.eHarlequin.com.

# ASSIGNMENT: SINGLE FATHER
*Caroline Anderson*

Double Destiny

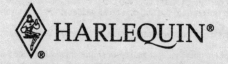

TORONTO • NEW YORK • LONDON
AMSTERDAM • PARIS • SYDNEY • HAMBURG
STOCKHOLM • ATHENS • TOKYO • MILAN • MADRID
PRAGUE • WARSAW • BUDAPEST • AUCKLAND

ISBN 0-373-03732-5

ASSIGNMENT: SINGLE FATHER

First North American Publication 2003.

Copyright © 2002 by Caroline Anderson.

**Printed in U.S.A.**

# CHAPTER ONE

'MISS WILLIAMS? It's Xavier Giraud. I gather from Jackie that you might still be interested in my vacancy.'

That gorgeous dark-chocolate voice again, rich and mellow, with the slight French accent that gave it an edge of mystery. Despite her exhaustion and disillusionment, something Fran had thought was dead and buried flickered into life.

'Yes—yes, that's right,' she replied. 'I'd like to talk to you again about it. I'm sorry if I sound indecisive, but it's so far from what I've done up to now and I do want to be sure before I make a commitment, for both our sakes.'

'Of course. I understand absolutely. It's rather a strange job—or rather, I suppose, a combination of jobs. Not many practice nurses work as nanny-cum-housekeeper as well, but don't let me put you off, for heaven's sake!'

His soft chuckle tingled over her nerve endings and brought them zinging to attention.

'So, when could you come and see me again?' he went on. 'Are you in London at the moment?'

'No—no, I'm up here now for good,' she said, fingers crossed, wondering if it was true. She'd like it to be, but she did need somewhere to live, of course, and fast. She couldn't camp on Jackie's floor indefinitely.

'Right. So you could be available at short notice?

5

It's just that I'm stuck for cover for the children at the moment, and I'm having to take the afternoons off, and it's really not fair on my colleagues.'

There was the slightest hesitation before he added, 'You do know, by the way, that my daughter doesn't walk or talk, I take it? Jackie did tell you?'

'She did mention it,' Fran said guardedly. Actually, Jackie had said a great deal more when she'd told Fran about the post Xavier had asked her agency to fill, but Fran wasn't about to repeat any of it to him. She'd wait and see for herself just how forthcoming he was about the circumstances behind his daughter's accident.

'And that's not a problem?'

'Not to me,' she said, crossing her fingers and hoping she wasn't being too hopelessly optimistic. 'I assume I won't be expected to carry her up and down stairs?'

'No, of course not,' he assured her hastily. 'She can transfer from chair to stairlift and bed and so on without help, and she bathes and dresses herself pretty much unaided.'

There was a pause, and she could almost hear the cogs whirring. Then he spoke again.

'Look, I have an idea. I'm tied up at the moment, but I'd like to see you as soon as possible. Could you get here for the end of surgery? About elevenish? We could have a chat, and I can show you round and introduce you to the others, and then, if I can persuade someone to do my calls, I could take you to my house and show you the setup. You won't be able to meet the children, of course, because they're at school until four o'clock, but it would be a start. What do you think?'

She hesitated for the merest instant, wondering how wise it was to involve herself with a widower and two motherless children, one of whom, according to Jackie, had been left with terrible, crippling injuries, not all of them physical.

Then she thought of working as a practice nurse, a quiet, orderly existence about as far removed from her work in A and E as it was possible to get, and dismissed her hesitation. Besides, she needed somewhere to live—fast.

'That would be fine, Dr Giraud. Shall I see you there at eleven o'clock?'

'That would be wonderful,' he said, and she thought she could hear relief in his voice. 'I look forward to seeing you again, Miss Williams.'

The line cut with a little click, and she replaced the receiver thoughtfully. Well, he seemed keen enough to see her again, and he'd come over as a very decent sort of person. She could do worse than look after him and his children and do a few inoculations.

She left the agency's little office tucked away behind Reception, and went through to tell Jackie about her imminent second interview and quiz her friend a little more about the man with the most fascinating voice she'd heard in years.

She didn't get a chance. There was someone else in there, a man she recognised—a man with a sexy, lopsided grin and the most arresting blue eyes she'd ever seen. He looked up at her and her heart lurched and then settled again. Good grief! Twice in ten minutes. She was going to develop chronic arrhythmia at this rate.

His smile widened in recognition. 'Well, if it isn't

the bodacious Sister Williams,' he said, and Fran suppressed a smile.

'Well, if it isn't the accident-prone Mr Nicholson. It's good to see you alive.'

'Do you two know each other?' Jackie chipped in, clearly agog, and he chuckled.

'Let's just say we met over a red-hot needle a little while ago.'

'Yes. How is the chest?' Fran asked him, and he gave a short, humourless laugh.

'Oh, the chest is fine—it's healed beautifully. Unfortunately, though, the rest of me is lagging behind a little, hence my visit here. I need a nurse.'

Jackie smiled at her encouragingly, and Fran sat down, rapidly getting a sinking feeling that her friend wanted her to take this assignment instead of the one with Dr Giraud.

Not a chance. Whatever her reservations about working for the GP, they paled into insignificance compared to this. This man, with his panther grace and lazy, sexy eyes, was trouble, with a capital T, and she had no intention of getting involved.

Grin or no grin.

'I've got an interview at eleven with Giraud,' she said quietly but firmly.

Jackie waved her hand. 'You've got another one now,' she said, and Fran gave an inward sigh and looked at Josh more closely. The situation didn't improve with inspection.

He had fading bruises round his eyes, a cast on his arm and an external fixator on his leg. She asked him a few questions and didn't like the answers.

He'd had an accident twelve days before; that she'd known because of all the news coverage. What she hadn't known, and what he now told her, was the extent of his injuries, and it made an impressive list.

He'd had a blood clot removed from his brain, his liver and spleen had been damaged, his pelvis was cracked, his right wrist was broken, his right femur was pinned and the fixator on his lower right leg was holding together a collection of matchwood, from what she could gather.

Why he felt he was well enough to go home, she couldn't begin to imagine, but there was no way she was going with him, however beguiling the smile or challenging the eyes. It was altogether too close to her recent work in A and E—she could imagine the carnage at the site of the RTA, the flashing lights, the controlled pandemonium in Resus—no way. Much too close to home.

When the accident had happened, right in the middle of her crisis at work, it had been all the more shocking to see it on the news because she'd only just treated him. He'd fallen over a cat and landed on a binbag full of rubbish, cutting his chest. She'd teased him, and then a few days later he'd nearly died.

She shot Jackie a slightly desperate smile. 'Could we have a word?'

'Sure. Just a moment, Mr Nicholson. We'll soon have you sorted out.'

'Just so long as you don't leave me at the mercy of my mother,' he said with a thread of desperate laughter in his voice, and Jackie smiled and made soothing promising noises that Fran hoped didn't include her.

They went into the office and Jackie leant back against the door and rolled her eyes. 'Oh, he is so *gorgeous*!' she said under her breath. 'I can't believe you know him. You are going to take this job, aren't you? You're not going to be silly?'

Fran shook her head. 'No. I'm going to see Dr Giraud at eleven and I'm probably going to take his job—if he offers it to me. And I don't know Josh, I've only met him once.'

'Well, surely you know who he is? Good grief, he's famous.'

'Yes, they talked about him at work. I'd never heard of him,' Fran confessed. 'I gather he's got a bit of money.'

'A bit? I think the expression is "fabulously wealthy",' Jackie said with a chuckle. 'Anyway, what about the job? He needs looking after. It was a high-speed crash on the A12—something about a horse on the road. It was one of those really dark nights. Judging by the sound of it, he was very lucky to escape with his life. I'd forgotten all about it. Fran, it's the chance of a lifetime. You *have* to take the job!'

For a brief moment she hesitated, tempted by the glamour, the wealth—and that grin. Then she thought of Xavier Giraud, the man with the incredible voice and the tragic children, and she shook her head slowly.

'No. I don't think so, Jackie. It would just bring back too many memories. I've seen too many young men like him die. I don't need it.'

'He's not going to die.'

'Please, I can't. Anyway, I've said I'll see Dr Giraud. I can't go back on that. I'm sure you'll find a whole queue of young women happy to take Josh Nicholson on, and probably loads of older ones as well, come to that. And if all else fails, there's always his mother, by the sound of it.'

Jackie laughed softly. 'Never mind the older ones and his mother, I might have to come out from behind the desk and look after him myself—if I hadn't just met David, I might well be tempted.' She squeezed Fran's shoulder and smiled forgivingly.

'You go and see your Dr Giraud. He's lovely, too, in fact. Not as rich, and there are the kids, of course, but he's a super guy. He's got the nicest eyes, and all the patients are in love with him.'

'Even the men?' Fran said drily, then laughed. 'Don't answer that. You go and sort out Mr Nicholson, and I'll go round to the surgery now. I'll be a few minutes early, but I want to be sure of finding a parking place. I'll let you know how I get on.'

She went through the back to the agency's tiny car park and then debated walking along to the surgery for all of three seconds before she slid behind the wheel of her little car and eased out into the road. She'd had precious little sleep last night, what with one thing and another, and the last thing she felt like doing was racing along the quay to the surgery and arriving windswept and flustered for her interview. She looked bad enough already!

It was further by car because of the one-way system, but the traffic was quiet, as it usually was on a weekday morning in sleepy Woodbridge, and she drove slowly down through the winding streets of the little town to the surgery.

It was housed in a purpose-built complex near the quay, modern and well equipped, and she arrived with minutes to spare. Still, better early than late.

The surgery car park was almost full and for a couple of seconds she regretted her impulse to drive, but she just managed to squeeze her car into a tiny space at the end next to the wall. Not for the first time, she was thankful her car was small. It certainly made life easier.

Locking up, she went into the reception area and rang the bell. A pleasant woman in her thirties with a welcoming smile and a friendly manner came out and asked how she could help. She had a name badge on that said she was Sue Faulkner, Receptionist, and Fran returned her smile.

'Hi. I'm Fran Williams—I've got an interview with Dr Giraud when he's finished his surgery,' she said, and the woman's smile widened.

'Ah, you're the nurse! Come on in. I'm afraid he's still got patients, but I'll make you a cup of coffee while you wait. I could have warned you not to bother to be early, he's always running late. He likes to give the patients a thorough hearing, so he always has too many because they all want him, and he always over-runs. Still, it'll give you a chance to meet the rest of us. I gather you were here last Friday?'

'Yes, that's right,' Fran told her. 'I didn't see you then.'

'No, you wouldn't, I don't work on Fridays. Still, I've met you now. Angie's here, the full-time practice nurse, so she can show you round, I'm sure, and tell you a bit more. Come on through.'

While she was talking she lifted up a flap in the counter and opened the gate under it, and Fran followed her into the back of the reception area and through to the office.

It was a hive of activity, but nevertheless everyone turned and smiled a welcome, and the practice nurse put down the pile of supplies she was carrying and came over, her hand extended.

'Hi, again. Everybody, this is Francesca Williams—our new team member, with any luck.'

'Fran,' she said with a laugh, 'and I'm not counting my chickens.'

'Oh, nonsense. You haven't run screaming yet, that's better than the others. Come and see the room you'll be working in, and then we'll have a coffee. Xavier'll be ages, I expect.'

She followed Angie out through the waiting room and down a corridor, her words echoing in her head. Run screaming? From what? She felt a quiver of doubt and wondered what on earth Jackie had let her in for.

'Why should they run screaming?' she asked, but Angie just laughed and shut the door of the treatment room behind them.

'Oh, you know—mention kids and people either love them or hate them. So far everybody's either hated them or had their own after-school commitments. Most people who want to work part time in the morning have kids of their own, or else they just want to dabble. Nobody wants to take on a disabled kid, and hardly anybody wants to live in, or at least not for the right reasons.'

Fran shrugged, wondering if being homeless was a good enough reason. 'I haven't got anywhere to live at the moment, so it suits me, at least on a temporary basis. I've only just moved back to the area.' Very only just, she added to herself—about twelve hours ago, to be exact, but Angie didn't need to know that.

The other woman cocked her head on one side and studied Fran thoughtfully. 'You do know it's a permanent job, don't you?'

Fran nodded. 'Yes—but I was told he needed

someone now regardless and would take me on a temporary basis if necessary.'

Angie sighed and nodded. 'Well, that's certainly true. He's run ragged, trying to cope with work and the children, and we're certainly at full stretch here. I'm sorry, I can't remember what Xavier said about you. Have you worked as a practice nurse before?'

'No,' Fran confessed. 'I was an A and E sister until ten days ago.'

'Oh, gosh, well, you're going to be bored to death here, then,' Angie said with a humourless laugh. 'I'm afraid we can't offer you drama and excitement.'

'Good. I've had enough drama and excitement to last me a lifetime.' She could see a question forming in Angie's eyes, and cut it off deftly. 'Will I need to train for this job?'

'Yes—but I can do it as you go along. It's not a problem. It's just a pain having to keep retraining new people every few weeks, but it can't be avoided and at least you're up to speed with current treatment.'

'Well, I'm good with first aid.' Fran chuckled. 'But I don't suppose I know the first thing about leg ulcers.'

'Easy. I'll make sure you get lots of help. I'm always here in the mornings, so you won't have to struggle. So, this is the room. Nothing flashy like you're used to, I don't suppose. Where did you work, Ipswich?'

'No—London,' Fran said, looking round and being deliberately uncommunicative. She didn't want to go into her reasons with the delightful but very open Angie, at least not until she'd spoken to Dr Giraud again and knew she was at least going to be offered the job.

'Tell me about the equipment you use,' she said, deliberately focusing on the here and now, and for a few minutes they chatted about procedures while Angie showed her some of the more sophisticated kit at their disposal.

Then the door opened, and Fran turned to see who had come in and her heart skidded to a halt.

'Ah, Xavier, I was just showing Fran the room,' Angie was saying, but she was hardly aware of the other woman's voice. Instead she was transfixed once again by the haunting quality of those smoke-grey eyes that seemed to be searching deep into her soul. A smile creased their corners, and she thought she'd never seen a kinder pair of eyes in her life.

'Miss Williams, I'm so sorry to keep you waiting. It was just one of those days. In fact, they're all one of those days,' he confessed with a wry smile, and held out his hand. 'It's good to meet you once more.'

That voice again—and she'd forgotten what a physical presence he had. He was tall, a shade over six feet, perhaps, with thick, springy hair and shoulders wide enough to lean on. His mouth was full and chiselled, his jaw strong, and there was enough character in his face for ten men.

'It's good to see you, too,' she said, placing her hand in his. His fingers curled around the back of hers, warm and firm and confident, yet gentle at the same time, and she felt an inexplicable sense of homecoming.

'Come on through to my consulting room—we can have a chat in peace. Have they offered you coffee?'

'I was about to make it,' Angie said, and he smiled at her.

'You couldn't make two and bring them through

for us, could you? I've only got a few minutes, I've got a call to go out on—it's not that urgent, I don't think, but I want to be sure.'

'OK, two it is.'

Fran followed him through the corridor and he ushered her through a door into his consulting room. It was bright and modern and well equipped, and there were pictures on the wall behind his desk which she hadn't noticed on Friday.

His family, of course. A boy and a girl, and a woman, probably his wife, small and dainty and much more chic than Fran could ever be.

So what? she thought unconvincingly. You aren't trying to compete with her.

He opened his mouth to speak and the phone rang. He gave a barely audible sigh and excused himself, then lifted the receiver.

It was obvious from the conversation that his patient was deteriorating, and he glanced at his watch and sighed again, ramming a hand through his hair. A tousled strand fell over his forehead and he pushed it back impatiently.

'OK. Tell Mrs Donaldson I'll come now and see him, and ask Stuart to take my other calls, please,' he said, and turned to Fran with an apology in his eyes. 'I'm sorry,' he began, but she shrugged.

'That's the way it is. Why don't I come with you, and we can talk while you drive?'

Relief washed over his face. 'Would you?' he said, and she wondered if he was afraid to let her go without her signing on the dotted line, if what Angie had said about the other candidates was true.

'Of course,' she said. 'You can't keep your patient waiting.'

His brow pleated thoughtfully. 'It sounds as if it could be a GI bleed, but she's a bit of a worrier, so it may not be. He hasn't been suffering with gastric problems that I'm aware of, but that doesn't mean anything. Still, I won't know till I see him, so if you're OK to come with me, we'll go now. It's a short way out of town, so we'll have a few minutes to talk at least.'

He stood up and opened the door, just as Angie appeared with two cups of coffee.

'Sorry, I have to go out and I'm taking Fran with me,' he said with a rueful smile at her.

'No worries, I'm sure I can find a home for it,' Angie replied, and the look on her face suggested that it wasn't the first time.

Just like A and E, Fran thought. Every time you thought you had a minute, something would happen. They picked up their coats from Reception and she followed him out to the car park. He had a people carrier, not the huge sort but easier than an ordinary car to get his disabled daughter in and out of, she imagined.

He threw his coat onto a back seat, slid behind the wheel and started the engine, fastening his seat belt as he pulled out of the car park. 'I'm sorry about the coffee,' he said as they drove off, but she just shrugged.

'It doesn't matter, I'm used to it. It happens all the time in A and E.'

'That's what you did before, isn't it? Work in A and E?'

'Yes.' She didn't elaborate, but as she'd expected he didn't let it go.

'Tell me about it,' he said, and, although it was a question and not an order, she felt she had no choice.

'I was a specialist trauma nurse. I did it for a couple of years.'

'And then?' he pressed, and she swallowed hard and straightened up.

'Then I gave up. I finished ten days ago.'

Even thinking about it made her feel sick, it was all still so raw and fresh, like an open wound. She hugged her arms round herself and hoped he'd give up, but he didn't. He couldn't, of course, because he had to find out about her. That was what her interview was all about, and she'd known it was coming, so she just braced herself and waited.

'So recently? Forgive me for saying this, but it seems strange that you should leave when you had no other job lined up. Was it a sudden decision?'

'Pretty much.'

He paused, then said cautiously, 'May I ask why?'

No, she wanted to scream, but she couldn't. Instead she shrugged. He had to know, in case it happened again. 'It just happened one day. I just froze up,' she said bluntly. 'I suppose if you want a technical term for it, you could call it burnout. Whatever, I couldn't do it any more, and after a few days, I had to stop.'

He nodded his understanding. 'I'm sorry, that's tough. It does happen, though. In all branches of medicine, I suppose, but especially on the front line. Sometimes it just gets too much, doesn't it?' he said, and suddenly she found herself telling him all about it, about the blood and the waste of life and the endless failures, day after day, even though it was never their fault.

'We had a run of fatalities,' she told him. 'One

after another, all young, all foolish, all so unnecessary. I just realised between one patient and the next that I couldn't go and talk to another set of bereaved parents and try and make sense of it for them where none could be made. I just couldn't do it any more.'

'So what happened?'

'My boss sent me home, but the next day wasn't any better, or the one after that, so he told me to go away and think about it, and he'd have me back when I was sorted, if ever. I don't know if I'll ever be ready to go back, though. It's only ten days ago, but it feels like a lifetime, and I don't think I'll ever be able to do it again. And now I just feel so lost. I thought I knew what I was doing with my life, and now suddenly I don't, and I don't know what's going to happen.'

She shrugged again, just a tiny shift of her shoulders, but he must have caught the movement out of the corner of his eye because he shot her an understanding smile.

'It's hard when everything seems to be going smoothly and then fate throws a spanner in the works. I know all about that and the effect it can have on you.'

She closed her eyes and groaned inwardly. Oh, what an idiot! 'I'm so sorry,' she said. 'I didn't mean it to come out like that. It's nothing like as bad as what's happened to you and your children, and I didn't mean to imply—'

'You didn't. It was me that drew the parallel, and it does exist. In my case it was a bit more dramatic, but yours is no less valid. Life-changing moments are usually pretty drastic, by definition. Let's just hope we aren't going to find one here.'

He swung into a driveway and cut the engine, and Fran followed him up the path of a neat little bungalow. The front door was open by the time they reached it, and the elderly woman waiting for them was wringing her hands with worry.

'Oh, Dr Giraud,' she said, clutching his arm. 'Oh, he's worse. He looks all grey and waxy—come in.'

Fran followed them down the hall to a bedroom at the back. An elderly man was lying in bed, his skin every bit as grey and waxy as Mrs Donaldson had said, and Fran took one look at him and her heart sank. He was obviously hypovolaemic and shocky, and his condition was all too familiar.

Please, no, she thought. Don't let him bleed to death. Not the first patient I'm involved with.

'Mr Donaldson, tell me about the pain,' Dr Giraud said, quickly taking his blood pressure and pulse, scanning him with eyes that Fran sensed missed nothing.

'It's just here,' he said, pointing to his midsection. 'So sore. It's been getting worse for days.'

'Any change in bowel habits? Change of colour of stools?'

'Black,' he said weakly. 'I read about that somewhere. That's blood, isn't it?'

Xavier nodded. 'Could well be. I think you've got a little bleed going on in there. Fran, could you get a line in for me?' he asked, turning towards her and giving her a reassuring smile. 'A large-bore cannula and saline to start. I'm going to phone the ambulance station and bring the oxygen in from the car. Are you OK to do that?'

'Sure,' she said, quelling her doubts, and found the necessary equipment in his bag. Part of her interview, or just another pair of qualified hands? Whatever, within moments the line was in, she was running in the saline almost flat out and checking his blood pressure again with the portable electronic monitor.

'What is it?' Xavier asked, coming back in just as the cuff sighed and deflated automatically.

'Ninety over fifty-two.' It had been ninety over fifty-six before, she'd noticed, so it was falling too fast for comfort.

He frowned. 'OK, I've told them to have some O-neg standing by. We'd better take some blood for cross-matching and a whole battery of other tests while we wait for the ambulance, because once they start the transfusion it'll be useless. Could you do that for me? There are bottles in my bag.'

He turned to the patient. 'Right, Mr Donaldson, let's put this mask on your face and give you some oxygen, it'll help you breathe more easily.'

Once that was done he sat on the edge of the bed and explained to them what was happening and what Fran was doing.

'The ambulance is on its way—Mrs Donaldson, could you find him some pyjamas and wash things to take with him? They'll be here in a minute and you don't want to hold them up.'

'Of course not. I'll get everything ready.'

She started going through drawers, clearly flustered and panicked, and Mr Donaldson watched her worriedly.

'Betty, not those, the blue ones,' he said as she pulled out his pyjamas, and while he was distracted Fran caught Xavier's eye.

'I'll check his BP again,' he murmured, and while she labelled her blood bottles he repeated the test. It was eighty-seven over forty-eight, and he winced almost imperceptibly. Only a slight drop, but in a very short time, she thought, so the fluids weren't holding him stable.

'Open it right up,' he said quietly, indicating the saline with a slight movement of his head. 'I'll call the ambulance station again, ask them to hurry. I've spoken to the surgical reg on call and told him to stand by, but there's not much else we can do here.'

An endless five minutes later the ambulance arrived, and Mr Donaldson and his worried wife were whisked away, leaving Fran and Xavier standing on the drive watching them go.

They didn't speak. There was nothing much to say. They both knew it was touch and go, and Mr Donaldson was already weakened from the slow and steady blood loss he'd suffered over the last few days.

Reaction set in, and Fran's legs started to tremble. She didn't think he'd noticed, but once they were in the car and driving back towards Woodbridge, Xavier shot her a weary smile.

'Bit close for comfort, eh?' he said softly, and she swallowed and nodded.

'I thought it would be easier—less cutting edge.'

'It is—or your part of it is under normal circumstances. Don't forget, you wouldn't usually have been there. Still, I'm glad you were with me. I needed that extra pair of hands, and you got the line in amazingly fast considering his low pressure. Thanks for that. Thanks for all your help, in fact, you were great.'

Odd, how those few words of praise and thanks could make her feel so very much better. She'd done nothing she hadn't done hundreds of times before, but to have gained his approval was somehow extraordinarily uplifting.

She put Mr Donaldson firmly to the back of her mind, settled back against the seat and let the tension drain away. 'So where to now?' she asked after a minute.

'My house. We can have coffee without interruption, I can show you the accommodation which goes with the job and if we get really lucky we might even find time for some lunch.'

'Sounds good,' she said, realising she was starving hungry.

'And then,' he added with a grin, 'if I still haven't managed to put you off, you can meet the children.'

## CHAPTER TWO

THE house was wonderful. It was situated in one of the best parts of town, the gateway set in a high brick wall, and as Xavier swung in off the road, Fran's breath caught in her throat.

The house was Georgian, built of old Suffolk White bricks that had mellowed to a soft greyish cream, and with a typically Georgian observance of symmetry it had a porticoed front door in the centre and tall windows each side. Across the upper floor, just like a child's drawing, were three more windows nestled under the broad eaves of the pitched and hipped roof, but unlike a child's drawing the proportions were perfect.

Despite the elegance of the house, it wasn't so grand that it was intimidating. It looked homely and welcoming, the garden a little on the wild side, and the fanlight over the front door was echoed in the sweep of gravel in front of the house on which he came to rest.

One thing was sure, she realised. It might not be intimidatingly grand, but he hadn't bought this house on a doctor's salary, not unless he had a thriving and possibly illegal private practice!

He ushered her through the door into a light and gracious entrance hall, and Fran tried to keep her mouth shut so her chin didn't trail on the ground. It was *gorgeous*.

The floor was laid in a diamond chequer-pattern of

24

black and white tiles, and on the far side the staircase rose in a graceful curve across a huge window that soared up to the ceiling on the upper floor.

The simple beauty of the staircase was marred by the presence of a stairlift, but apart from that and the ramp by the steps to the front door, it was just as it had been built, she imagined.

The doorways were wide, the rooms large enough to accommodate a wheelchair with ease, and as she followed him through to the kitchen at the back, she felt a pang of envy. She'd always loved houses like this, always dreamed of living in one, and here he was owning it, the lucky man.

Then she caught sight of another photograph of his wife amidst all the clutter on the old pine dresser in the kitchen, and the envy left her, washed away by guilt and sympathy.

Lucky? No, she had no reason to envy him. The house was just bricks and mortar, and living in it were three people whose lives had been devastated by their loss. How could she possibly have envied them that?

Xavier was patting the dogs, two clearly devoted and rather soppy Labradors, and when he'd done his duty he turned to her.

'Are you OK with dogs? I forgot to mention them.'

'I'm fine. I grew up with Labs. Come on, then, come and make friends.'

They did, tongues lolling, leaning on her legs and grinning up at her like black bookends, one each side. 'You soppy things,' she said to them, and their tails thumped in unison.

'The thin one's Kate, the fatter one with the grey muzzle is Martha, her mother. Just tell them to go and lie down when you've had enough. Shall I put the kettle on?'

Fran straightened up and grinned at him. 'That sounds like the best thing I've heard in hours. I could kill a cup of tea.'

He chuckled. 'Ditto. And while it boils, I'll put the dogs out for a minute and then show you the flat.'

He went through a door at the back of the kitchen into a lobby and opened the outside door to let the dogs out, then turned back to her with a smile. 'Right, you need to be careful, the stairs are a little steep.'

She followed him through a door in the corner of the lobby that led to the narrow, winding back stairs, and at the top they came out onto a little landing in what must have been the servants' quarters. To the left, its ceilings atticky and low, was a small but comfortable sitting room overlooking the garden; to the right was a bedroom with a double bed under a quilted bedspread, all whites and creams and pretty pastels.

Fran looked around her in slight disbelief and felt a lump in her throat.

'Oh, it's gorgeous,' she murmured.

'There's a bathroom there, and a tiny kitchen so you can be independent if you want. And through here is the rest of the house.'

He opened a door at the end of the landing and went through it onto the much larger landing at the head of the main stairs. There was a wheelchair parked by the stairlift, in readiness, Fran imagined, for his daughter's return, and she could see through the open doors into their bedrooms.

One was immaculate, one reasonably tidy, the last chaos.

'That's Nick's room,' Xavier said with a wry smile, indicating the messy one. 'This one's Chrissie's.'

He pushed open the door of the reasonable one, and she looked around it, at all the pictures of horses and boy bands and other images dear to the heart of a young teenager, and she wondered what Chrissie was like and what had really happened.

'Tell me about her,' she said softly, and he sighed and tunnelled his fingers through his hair.

'She's…complicated,' he said slowly. 'She's in a wheelchair, and she doesn't speak, but they can't find anything wrong with her. They've done a million tests and can't detect anything, and she moves and talks in her sleep, but when she's awake, she just won't communicate—well, not a great deal. She has a little hand-held computer that she uses for important stuff, but mostly she doesn't bother. And it's not that she can't, because she's doing fine at school, even without speaking. There's nothing wrong with her academically. It's bizarre.'

'Was she badly hurt in the accident?'

'No. Nick had a broken arm, and Sara was killed instantly, but Chrissie was untouched. That's the odd thing about it. She's seen therapists and psychiatrists and every other sort of ''ist'', but nobody's found the key. She's locked in there, and I can't let her out, and I'm a doctor, for God's sake!'

He broke off and turned away, his voice choked, and Fran lifted her hand to touch him, to reach out to him. She didn't, though. She let it fall to her side, because there was nothing she could say to make it right, nothing she could do to make it better.

Well, only one thing.

'If you were hoping to put me off, you've failed,' she said softly.

Xavier turned, a flicker of hope in his anguished eyes, and his mouth kicked up in a crooked smile. 'Well, so far, so good. Of course, you haven't met them yet.' He looked down, studying his hand as it rested on Chrissie's doorknob, and then looked up at her again.

'I really am in a bit of a fix with this at the moment. I don't suppose there's any way I could talk you into taking it on immediately, even just temporarily, at least the domestic side? I'm more than happy with your nursing skills, but this week I'm stuck completely on the domestic front unless I can get some help, and I can't expect you to take us on without trying it. Would you consider a week's trial? Give the kids a chance, give me a chance? And if you hate it, maybe I can find someone else...'

He finally ground to a halt, the flicker of hope fading in his eyes as she watched. He thought she was going to refuse, she realised. Well, she wasn't.

'That sounds fine,' she said, and his eyes fell for a moment. When he raised them to her face the hope was back, hope and relief in equal proportions.

'Thank you,' he said fervently, then he dragged in a deep breath and pulled himself together visibly.

'Right, now that's sorted, how about that cup of tea? And if you're really unlucky, I might even cook you lunch.'

They went back to the surgery after lunch, Xavier to his antenatal clinic, Fran to acquaint herself further with Angie and familiarise herself with the room she would be working in from the following morning. At

three-thirty promptly, Xavier came into the office
where she was talking to Angie about her routine.

'I'm going to collect the children from school. Do
you want to come? It would help you to see it at first
hand, before you have to do it yourself.'

'Good idea,' she agreed, and wondered why she
hadn't thought of it. Lack of sleep, she decided, or
just plain shell-shock.

She went with him out to the car park, noticing for
the first time that his people carrier had a rear seat
missing, presumably where Chrissie would go in her
wheelchair. The enormity of what she was taking on
suddenly sank in, and she felt a little flutter of doubt
about her ability to do this part of the job.

She must be crazy, she thought. She didn't know
the first thing about looking after children of that
age—except, of course, that she'd been thirteen once
and had had a younger brother, so she knew all about
the dynamics of that! But—Chrissie?

Still, she had no choice. It was a job, it was a home,
albeit perhaps only for a week, and with a steadying
breath she put the doubts aside.

If Xavier was prepared to take her on, she'd give
it a go, at least for this trial period. She knew enough
about children to cope for that long, and, besides,
Chrissie had problems. Maybe she could help get to
the root of them. She'd certainly give it her best shot,
although if the girl's own father had failed, it seemed
unlikely that a total stranger could do better.

Except, of course, that it was often easier for an
outsider to see the situation clearly.

'I phoned the hospital, by the way,' he was saying
as he drove. 'Bernard Donaldson's made it through
surgery—he had a perforated duodenal ulcer.'

Fran dragged her mind back to the earlier events of the day and nodded. 'Figures. I'm glad he's OK. They seemed a sweet couple.'

'They are—truly devoted. Hopefully he'll be all right now. OK, we're at the school. You need to go through this set of gates, not the ones further down, so you can get right up to the school to collect them. Otherwise you can't get close enough.'

Xavier went slowly along the drive and over the speed ramps, parked the car, and then they waited. Children were pouring out of the school, running and pushing and laughing, heading in their droves for the bus pull-in, others going down the drive to their parents, and then the crowd cleared like mist and she saw them.

A slender girl in a wheelchair, her hair hanging long and blonde around her shoulders, her trousers dangling on skinny legs, she looked tired and defeated.

Behind her was a boy the spitting image of Xavier, with a big smile and untidy hair. His shirt was untucked on one side, his tie was hanging askew, his face was grubby, but he looked bright and cheerful and disgustingly healthy in contrast to his frail older sister.

He was pushing the wheelchair towards them, and Xavier went over to them and hugged him, bending to kiss his daughter's cheek. She didn't respond, just sat there expressionless, and Fran felt the flicker of doubt return in force.

Give her time, she thought, but the girl was looking straight through her as she stood there beside the car, waiting.

'Children, this is Miss Williams,' he said. 'She's

going to stay with us for a while and help me look after you.'

'Can you cook?' Nick asked her directly, and she laughed.

'Most things. It depends what you want.'

'Pizza—and Chrissie likes spag. bol.'

Fran nodded thoughtfully, transferring her gaze to the unresponsive girl. 'I think I can manage that.'

Chrissie looked away dismissively, and Fran thought that even without words she managed to communicate her feelings—and just now, her feelings were less than friendly.

'She's vegetarian, though,' Nick was adding. 'So no meat, worse luck. She doesn't do meat.'

'I'm sure Miss Williams knows what a vegetarian is, Nick,' Xavier put in drily, and opened the side door of the car. 'Fran, this board slides out of the floor like this, and locks, and then you can push the chair up and it clips into place.'

He pulled and clicked and then wheeled Chrissie effortlessly into the car, then with a clunk her chair was secure and he was sliding the board home and closing the door.

Fran decided to practise with the empty wheelchair before she had to do it for real. She didn't want to mess up and dump Chrissie on the drive, and she was sure Xavier would be less than thrilled, too, not to mention Chrissie herself!

Nick was piling all their bags into the back and climbing into the seat behind Xavier, chattering nineteen to the dozen about what he'd done and the goal he'd scored in football and that he needed new football boots and could he go on the field trip in February to France, and Harry had been kicked in the chin and had to go to hospital after football because his jaw might be broken.

Finally he ground to a halt, and Xavier shot Fran a wry glance. Still not put off? it seemed to say, but in truth she thought Nick was delightful, just a normal, healthy boy bursting with energy.

Chrissie, on the other hand, was almost unnerving with her silent watchfulness, and Fran wondered how on earth she would communicate with her. The hand-held computer would surely have its limitations, but she'd just watch Xavier and see how he did it, and then talk to him later after the children were in bed.

She'd already established to herself that Chrissie could convey her feelings. It was her needs that were more of an issue here, and of more concern to Fran. She didn't need to be liked. She did, however, need to be able to do her job, and she was on a week's trial. The last thing she wanted was to screw up yet another job.

Xavier couldn't believe his luck. He'd actually found someone—and not just anyone, but a highly skilled professional who by a freak of fate needed a live-in post, just when he was getting desperate.

He wouldn't trust Chrissie to an amateur—he couldn't. There was too much at stake, and a nurse of Fran's experience would be alert to any slight change in her. Not that it was likely, after all this time, but he still wasn't sure he really believed there was nothing wrong, and all the time he felt as if he was waiting for the other shoe to drop.

But Fran—Fran was a gift from the gods, and he hardly dared believe it. He'd phoned her old boss at the London hospital and had received such a glowing reference that he daren't tell her about it because she'd be so embarrassed. It seemed a tragic shame that her career in trauma had been cut short, but he wasn't complaining, not if it meant she was free to work for him.

He went into his study, the dogs in tow, and dropped into the chair behind his desk, swinging his feet up onto the worn and battered top and resting his head against the high leather back of the chair with a sigh.

He had some phone calls to make and one or two bits of paperwork to deal with, but he just wanted to grab a few precious, quiet minutes to himself. The children were tucked up in bed, the television was finally silenced and Fran was unpacking her possessions in her flat.

He closed his eyes and pictured her, those beautiful blue-grey eyes that said so much, bare lips the colour of a faded rose, full and soft and ripe. There was something incredibly English about her looks, the pale alabaster of her skin, the warm glow in her cheeks, the fine cheekbones. Her hair had been up, the dark, gleaming tresses scraped back into a loose knot and secured at her nape with a clip.

It made his fingers itch. He'd wanted to remove the clip, to free her hair and watch it fall in a curtain around her shoulders, to thread his fingers through it and touch the softness.

He'd wanted all sorts of things, like the feel of her body against him, the taste of her mouth on his tongue, the slide of her skin against his own, but he would never know these things.

She was an employee, a member of his team at work, a pivotal part of his home life, please, God, and he needed her in that capacity far more than he needed the mere gratification of his sexual desires. He'd managed without since Sara had died, and he could manage for as long as it took to sort Chrissie out.

Maybe then he'd allow himself the luxury of an affair—if he could find anyone stupid enough to take him on.

With a short sigh he swung his feet to the ground and went out to the kitchen, pouring himself a glass of wine from the bottle in the fridge. It was nothing special, just a supermarket cheapie that he'd picked up the other day, but it was cool and refreshing and it might blur the edges a bit, if he was lucky.

Not a chance. Fran came down the back stairs and through the door, her hair down around her shoulders, wearing jeans and a simple sweater that hugged her waist and showed off the soft, ample fullness of her breasts, and desire slammed through him like an express train.

Dear God. He was going to have to live with this woman, work with her, share almost every detail of his life with her.

Mere sexual gratification? *Mere?* He set his glass down with exaggerated care and forced himself to meet her eyes. 'Wine?'

'Oh, lovely, thanks. Actually, I wanted to talk to you about the children, particularly Chrissie, and I wouldn't mind a lesson in pulling out that ramp thing and clipping in the wheelchair, if you can be bothered.'

'Sure,' he said, glad to have something positive to focus on apart from the gentle swell of her breasts and the way her hair fell in those soft, shining waves across her shoulders. He pictured it spread out over a pillow, and stifled a groan. 'Let's go and do that now before it gets even colder,' he said, and, shrugging on his coat, he grabbed his car keys off the fridge and headed for the door, collecting the wheelchair as he went.

He seemed a little abrupt, Fran thought. Tired and preoccupied, perhaps? Worried about the children?

All of the above, probably. She hurried after him, practised slotting the ramp in and out and clipping in the wheelchair until she was sure she could do it blindfolded, and then they went back inside and he poured her the glass of wine he'd promised her and picked up his own.

'Let's go into my study,' he said. 'It's comfortable, and there's no danger of being overheard by the children.'

She nodded and followed him yet again. She seemed to have spent a great deal of time doing that today, she thought, but it was quite an interesting view, one the dogs must be quite used to as well. She stifled a smile and went into his study after him, the dogs trotting along beside her, and closed the door softly behind them all.

It was a lovely room, the walls completely lined with books, a battered desk of some considerable vintage set at right angles to the big, low window overlooking the drive. There was a huge leather swivel chair behind the desk and a toning leather chesterfield beside the fireplace.

Shoving the dogs off onto the floor, Xavier dropped into the chesterfield, waved at the other end of it and watched her as she settled into the other corner, a brooding look on his face.

She wondered what she'd done wrong, but apparently it was rather what she'd done right.

'You have no idea how grateful I am to you for stepping into this post with so little warning,' he said quietly. 'I was at my wits' end. I'd literally run out of options, and the kids were going to have to come to the surgery by taxi and sit in the office till I'd finished every night. Can you imagine Nick sitting still for that long? He'd be murdered by the staff before the week was out.'

Fran could believe it. He was certainly a live wire, she thought, although she couldn't imagine Chrissie being any trouble if you could cope with the cold-shoulder treatment. She'd come in that evening, settled herself down at the kitchen table in silence and ploughed her way steadily through her homework.

Nick, on the other hand, had had to be retrieved from his bedroom and practically screwed to the chair by his exasperated father before he'd finally given in and opened his books.

'Tell me about that little computer thing Chrissie has,' Fran said, remembering how she'd communicated with her father and brother during the evening.

'Her palm? It's just that, a tiny computer that fits in her hand and means she can communicate without writing—well, she does write, simplified letters that the computer reads and then brings up into print on the small screen for us to see. It's slower, but it means she doesn't ever run out of paper and, besides, it's cool. It gives her street cred, and I suppose in her position that's important.'

Fran nodded slowly. 'Yes, I'm sure you're right.'

She hesitated, then plunged on regardless. 'I hate to bring it up again, but—do you have any idea what it might have been about the accident that made her stop talking?'

A shadow came over his face and he shook his head. 'No. None. To be honest, I've hardly discussed it with her. Every mention of it distressed her so much in the beginning that we just avoided it, and opinion is divided on the efficacy of counselling in post-traumatic stress disorder—if it is PTSD. I still don't know if I believe that. I can't believe a healthy, active teenager would deliberately confine herself to a wheelchair and restrict herself to immobility and silence, no matter how traumatised.'

'What do the experts think?' she asked, curious as to their opinions, but he just laughed, a humourless, rather sad sound.

'Oh, the experts couldn't agree. Some wanted to try pressing her, forcing the issue; others said it was profoundly dangerous and she'd come out of it in time on her own. So what do you do? Who do you believe?'

'What *did* you do?'

Xavier shrugged. 'Nothing helped. The therapy made her even more withdrawn, so we stopped it and we just manage the situation as well as we can. She sees a physio twice a week and I do resisted exercises with her every evening, and she goes swimming on her games afternoon at a special hydrotherapy session, and I just hope to God she comes out of it before her body's permanently damaged.'

He looked down into his wineglass, his face taut, a muscle working in his jaw, and Fran had an overwhelming urge to take the glass out of his hand and lay him down and massage the tension out of his shoulders. He was like a bowstring, she thought, strung so tight he would break, and she wondered if he ever did anything for himself, took any time to be himself and not a father or a doctor.

With one hand he was idly fondling the ear of one of the dogs, propped lovingly against his leg, and the other dog had her chin on his foot.

Such devotion. It wasn't hard to see how he inspired it, she thought. He was so kind, so generous with himself, so thoughtful. He'd brought her things in out of her car, the few pitiful possessions she'd brought with her from London, and put them upstairs in the pretty little flat that was her new home.

He'd found her some clean linen and helped her make up the bed, turned up the heating to air the rooms and then left her alone to settle in and count her blessings.

All this after he'd cooked for them all, fed the dogs, supervised homework and chivvied the children through their bedtime routine.

He must be so tired, she thought, so tired and stressed and worried. If her presence here helped him, regardless of what she could do for Chrissie, then she'd feel she'd done her job well.

Nick she wasn't worried about. Nick was a normal, healthy, well-balanced young boy, and he just needed keeping in order. Well, she could do that. She'd done it for years with her brother.

'May I ask you something?' he said quietly, and Fran looked up to find those lovely, haunted eyes studying her face.

'Of course.'

'If you were living in London, how come you're

looking for a job up here and haven't got anywhere to live?'

She'd wondered when it was coming, and thought of lying to him, but somehow she didn't want to. Anyway, she knew instinctively that he'd be easy to tell.

'After I stopped working at the hospital I just felt lost. I'd been wandering around aimlessly for days, and I spent yesterday in the park doing more of the same, thinking over your job offer and wondering what to do. I was on my way home because my boyfriend was coming round, and someone was knocked down in front of me in the middle of Camden High Street. And I froze.'

He made a sympathetic noise and she shrugged and carried on. 'Luckily someone else came along who could help him, so I don't have to have his death on my conscience, but by the time it was all over and I got back, I was late, of course.'

'And your boyfriend had got sick of waiting?'

She gave a strangled little laugh. 'You might say that. He was in bed with my flatmate.'

He said something under his breath in French that she thought was probably rude, and she gave him a wry grin.

'Quite. So I left. I flung my clothes and a few things into the car, and turned my back on my entire life. I didn't know where to go, because my parents don't live here any more. They live in Devon near my brother and his wife, and none of them have any spare room, so I headed up here and camped with Jackie and just hoped your job was still on offer. Jackie's an old friend from school and nurse training days, and I spent the night with her last night and went to work with her this morning.'

'And rang me again.'

'Yes. Then Josh Nicholson tried to talk me into working for him instead.'

Xavier frowned. 'Josh Nicholson? But he's still in hospital, surely? He nearly killed himself, just a few days ago.'

'Quite. Having seen him, I'm only too ready to believe that. Is he a patient of yours?'

'Yes—and, of course, a well-known public figure. The news was full of it. But, yes, as it happens, I believe he is a patient, though I've never had to see him except for inoculations for foreign holidays and so on. He's never been unwell that I'm aware of.'

'Oh. Well, he doesn't look so hot now, so you might want to stand by for an emergency call!'

He laughed under his breath, then his eyes locked on hers again. 'So this was only—yesterday, is that right, that you found the boyfriend and your flatmate together?'

She nodded slowly. 'Yes. It seems about three lifetimes ago.'

'Well, that might be a good thing. Hell, I'm sorry. Was it serious? With the boyfriend?'

She thought of Dan, frivolous and uncommitted, and shook her head. 'No. It might have been eventually, I suppose, but, then, probably not. I'm not sure he had what it takes to be serious, and I'm not into casual sex.' She smiled brightly and tried to inject some light humour into her voice. 'So, anyway, here I am, utterly free, and scared to death.'

She didn't fool him for an instant. Instead of laughing, as he was supposed to, he smiled understandingly. 'There's no need to be scared, Fran. You have a home now, and a job. How long you stay is up to you.'

She nodded again, and to her disgust her eyes filled. She looked away, blinking hard to banish the too-ready tears. 'Thank you,' she said, a trifle unsteadily. 'Thank you for everything.'

'My pleasure. More wine?'

She dredged up a smile. 'Do you know, I think I will. I don't suppose two glasses will kill me.'

'Probably not, although it's pretty awful,' he said with a chuckle. 'I just grabbed it in the supermarket on Sunday. I had a feeling this week would call for it.'

He eased himself off the sofa and the dogs were at his heels instantly. Fran wondered a trifle hysterically if she should fall into place behind them, and nearly laughed aloud.

She was losing it, she thought, and then inexplicably her eyes filled again. Don't be an idiot, she told herself, but the events of the past two weeks caught up with her in a rush, and she curled over on her side on the sofa, buried her face in a cushion and sobbed as if her heart would break.

She didn't hear Xavier come back, but then the sofa shifted under his weight and he was there for her.

'Ah, Fran,' his voice murmured, and then strong hands were on her shoulders, lifting her against his chest, and his arms were round her, rocking her slowly against him, holding her safe until the storm of weeping was over.

'I'm sorry,' she sniffed, and pulled away, scrubbing her nose on the back of her hand. 'What an idiot you must think I am.'

'You're not an idiot at all. Here,' he said, passing
her a tissue, and she blew her nose and scrubbed her
eyes and sniffed hard, burrowing back into the corner
of the sofa in an attempt to retrieve her dignity.

'Your shirt's all soggy,' she said unevenly, and he
just smiled, a slow, crooked smile that nearly reduced
her to tears again.

She was shredding the tissue, so he took it from
her and replaced it with the glass of wine, and she
took a gulp and dragged in a huge deep breath and
smiled.

'Thanks,' she said, her throat still clogged with
tears, but he just shrugged.

'Sometimes it's better to let go,' he said softly.
'You've had a lot to deal with. Now, drink up and
tell me what you like to eat, so I can go shopping
tomorrow. We can't have you starving to death.'

How odd. The day before she wouldn't have cared.
Now, suddenly, she did, and it was all down to him.

'I eat anything,' she told him truthfully. 'Usually
everything, in fact!'

'I'll see what I can do. I normally call in at the
supermarket on my way home for lunch, or do a big
shop with the kids at the weekend, which is always
a nightmare.'

'Can't I do that for you?' she offered, and he
shrugged.

'Well—if you want to. I can get you some cash.
Are you sure?'

She nodded. 'I've got hours between the end of my
work in the morning and picking the children up from
school, so it's not a problem. Do you come home for
lunch every day?'

He nodded. 'If I can, if there's time. It gives me a

little time alone to relax and think—unwind a bit.
Don't think you have to cook for me, though. I usually have beans on toast or something like that—
something quick.'

He couldn't have given her a bigger hint, she
thought. She made a mental note to keep out of his
way at lunchtimes. 'I'll make sure there are plenty of
things in the cupboard for you to choose from,' she
said, and wondered why she felt disappointed.

How silly. 'Right, can you tell me exactly what I
have to do each day with the children—in fact, could
you write it down so I have it in black and white
what's expected of me, so the kids won't pull the
wool over my eyes?'

He snorted softly. 'You obviously know kids.'

'I remember being one,' she corrected. 'A new
babysitter was a great opportunity not to be missed.
I don't suppose yours are any different.'

His smile was wry. 'No—and don't imagine
Chrissie's innocent either. She might look as if butter
wouldn't melt in her mouth, but really she can be just
as naughty as Nick, and she's more devious. Don't
get me wrong, she's not a bad girl, but she is a normal
one in many ways. Don't let her fool you.'

The warning rang in Fran's ears the following morning while she was rushing to get them ready for
school and get herself to the surgery in time.

So far, so good, she thought as she arrived only a
minute late. Considering the wrangling and chaos and
lost shoes and missing books, it was a miracle she
was here at all, she thought, and having to put the
people carrier into the tiniest space in the car park
was a bit scary.

She wasn't used to driving such a big car, and if it hadn't been for the lack of choice, she would have protested. She didn't know how Xavier had got to work either. She hadn't even thought about it, but he hadn't said anything. She wondered if he'd want to borrow her car rather than walk—because how would he do his house calls after surgery if he was on foot? Still, surely he would have thought of that?

Puzzled, she headed for the surgery entrance, and then noticed a silver sports car parked in his space, a low-slung, mean little machine, and she smiled to herself. So he had another car, the absolute antithesis of the people carrier. Interesting.

She went inside, apologised for her lateness and grabbed the notes for her morning's patients. She was wearing her old Sister's uniform of a royal blue dress, but she'd put on weight since she'd worn it. She hadn't needed it recently because the uniform in her hospital had changed to tunics and trousers and the dress had been flung in a drawer for the past two years, so she hadn't realised that it had become a little snug over the bust and hips.

Still, it would do until she got another one, she thought, and with all the running up and down she'd done this morning, she'd very likely lose weight anyway. Tugging it straight, she went through to her room, took a steadying breath and pressed the button for her first patient.

# CHAPTER THREE

'So, how did it go?'

Fran pulled a face at him and smiled. 'Well, apart from the fact that I was late, not so bad, I don't suppose.'

Xavier frowned at her. 'Late? What went wrong? Did you get lost?'

'*I* didn't. Everything else did—the homework, the shoes, the bag—you name it, it vanished. It's my fault, I probably didn't allow enough time because I was treating them like adults, instead of remembering that they're children. Still, it won't happen again—and it was only a minute.'

'One minute!' He chuckled. 'I wouldn't worry about that. I'm nearly always late, and a great deal more than a minute, by the time we've fiddled about and had all the usual dramas. I would write that one down as a success!'

Well, that was one worry out of the way, she thought, watching him hang his jacket on the back of the door. He stretched and yawned and, hooking out a chair from the table with his foot, he sat down, his legs stretched out in front of him and his hands locked behind his head.

'In fact, I would say it was a success all round. You have no idea how wonderful it was to get to work this morning on time and without having to panic about the traffic and how late I was going to be. It made so much difference.'

'Good,' Fran said, relieved that he seemed satisfied. 'That's why I'm here, after all. All we have to work on now is getting *me* to work on time.'

He laughed, apparently completely unconcerned. 'I shouldn't worry about it, you'll soon settle into the routine. I just nag them automatically.'

'Well, I suppose I'll just have to start doing that too, but it seemed a bit much on the first day.'

'Don't worry, you'll soon get into the swing of it, believe me,' he said drily. 'Have you had lunch?'

She shook her head. 'No, I haven't, but don't worry about me. I was just about to go shopping.'

Xavier's brow creased into a frown and he patted his pockets. 'I haven't given you any money yet, and I haven't got any on me.'

Fran, conscious of the fact that he wanted to be alone at lunchtime, shook her head hastily. 'Don't worry about it now. I was only going to buy a few things—just owe me.'

He frowned again and stood up and opened the fridge, staring into it as if for inspiration.

'I tell you what, why don't we have a cheese sandwich or something and then go shopping together?' He pulled his head out of the fridge and turned towards her, cheese in one hand, pickle in the other, an expectant look on his face.

She opened her mouth to argue, then shut it again. If he wanted to invite her to join him for lunch, she wasn't going to refuse. She was absolutely starving.

'Sounds good. Shall I make coffee?'

'I'd rather have tea. I've had three cups of coffee already this morning and I'll be pinging off the ceiling if I'm not careful. I try to avoid that, it makes the patients nervous.'

Suppressing a smile, she put the kettle on and got the mugs ready while he made the sandwiches, standing beside her at the worktop, not so close that she felt crowded but certainly close enough for her to be aware of him.

Who was she kidding? She would have been aware of him on the other side of a football pitch!

She watched his hands out of the corner of her eye, noticing the practised competence of his movements. Of course, the children took packed lunches to school, and making sandwiches was something he did every night of the week. He ought to be able to do it competently. She wondered what else he did competently with his hands, and felt the colour rising in her cheeks.

'Pickle?'

'Thanks—just a streak.' She dragged her attention off his competent, sexy hands and back to the tea, mentally chiding herself. What he looked like was absolutely nothing to do with her, and she had no business fantasizing about the feel of his hands on her body!

She took the proffered sandwich, handed him his tea and retreated to the table, kicking her overactive libido into touch. She had to live and work with the man, and the last thing either of them needed was her coming onto him like a frustrated teenager.

She bit into the sandwich and pickle squelched out of the side onto her lip. She flicked her tongue out to retrieve it, and as she glanced up she caught Xavier watching her. He looked away instantly, but not before she'd seen a glimmer of something that could have been hunger in his eyes.

Him, too? No, she was imagining it. There was no

way he would be interested in her. He was wealthy, successful, he could have whoever he wanted. According to Jackie, all his patients were in love with him. The same was probably true of all the women in his social circle.

She bit into the sandwich again, more carefully this time, and as she did so she pondered on the extent of his social circle. Maybe he didn't have one? Perhaps he was so busy with the children that there simply wasn't time for socialising.

In which case, he was probably lonely, but that still didn't necessarily mean he would be interested in her. Why would he? She couldn't even tolerate the profession she'd been trained for, she'd had to bottle out. She felt a huge sense of failure about that, a deep personal disappointment that even time would probably never quite take away.

And besides, there was Sara hovering in the background, slim and chic and petite. Interesting that the words that best described his dead wife should be French. No, she couldn't compete with Sara, who was enshrined in his memory and therefore beyond reproach.

Fran reminded herself that she shouldn't even be trying, and she was giving herself another silent lecture when his voice interrupted her.

'Tell me about your patients.'

She looked quickly up at him, and decided she must have completely imagined the hunger in his eyes. There was certainly no sign of it now. The expression in them was bland and dispassionate, disinterested even.

Odd, how disappointing that was. She dragged her mind back to the subject.

'My patients? You mean this morning?'

He nodded. 'Did you have any problems?'

'No. I wasn't very quick, because I had to find out where everything was, of course, but once I'd groped my way round all the equipment it was a bit better. I had to do a couple of ECGs, and several bloods and a few inoculations, but I imagine Angie took anything complicated. Either that or there wasn't anything complicated today.'

Xavier's mouth quirked into a wry smile. 'That's quite likely. I warned you yesterday, excitement like Bernard Donaldson's perforated duodenal ulcer isn't commonplace.'

'Thank goodness! I thought I was going to freeze up when you asked me to put that IV line in.'

'I know,' he said quietly. 'It wasn't meant to be a test, I just didn't think about it. I was pushed and I knew you could do it, and it was only afterwards that I realised it might have been a bit tough for you. I'm sorry about that.'

Fran shrugged. 'That's OK, I didn't really mind, and it needed doing quickly. I think if we'd been much later, he might have been in real trouble.'

'Absolutely.' Xavier glanced at his watch. 'We will be, too, if we don't get on with the shopping. I have to get back to the surgery to do my antenatal clinic at three, and it's after half past one already. Come on.'

He stood up, automatically slotting his mug and plate into the dishwasher and shrugging into his jacket. Fran hastily drained the dregs of her tea, put her crockery with his and grabbed her fleece off the back of the door.

'Who's driving?' she asked him as she followed him out.

He tossed his keys in the air and caught them. 'Me? I don't very often get to play in my toy.'

She grinned at him. 'Aren't you getting a little bit old for toys?'

His answering grin was cheeky, and wiped years off him. 'We're never too old for toys,' he said, 'especially not this sort.' He slid behind the wheel of his sports car, and she squirmed into the passenger seat, grateful that she'd changed into her jeans and wasn't still wearing a skirt.

Getting in and out of a sports car was an art she hadn't yet perfected, and with the amount of practice she'd been getting, it was an art she wasn't likely to perfect in this lifetime. Still, maybe that was all about to change.

She fastened her seat belt, put her head firmly on the headrest and prepared to be impressed.

She was, but not by the speed. Xavier obeyed the speed limit all the way through town, and it was only when he overtook a car on the bypass that she had any real idea of how powerful the car was. He still didn't exceed the speed limit, however, possibly because of their close proximity to the police headquarters, and possibly, she thought, because his wife had died in a car accident and so he had good reason to be careful.

Or maybe he was just a sensible and law-abiding person who obeyed the rules. There weren't many of them in the world, and Dan certainly didn't qualify. If Dan had obeyed the rules, she thought with irony, she wouldn't be here now.

Oddly enough, he'd probably done her a favour…

\*   \*   \*

Two hours later, Fran pondered on the wisdom of that thought. Nick was threatening to boil over, sliding away from the table to avoid his homework whenever her back was turned, and Chrissie was being silently obstructive.

She refused to communicate, and Fran was at her wits' end. Well, she thought, two can play at that game, and for the next hour she ignored the girl. Not only did she ignore her, she made sure that Nick wasn't available to run errands for her.

In the end, Chrissie took herself upstairs in a sulk, and Fran heaved a sigh of relief and frustration and concentrated on getting their supper. Vegetarian, of course, because Chrissie didn't do meat, and, however frustrated she might be by her, Fran had no intention of disregarding her principles.

'So, what's for supper?'

Nick was peering suspiciously into the pot, and she hid a smile. 'A vegetable and bean cottage pie,' she told him, and he shot her a look of disgust.

'No self-respecting shepherd would eat that,' he replied, the tone of his voice speaking volumes, and she vowed to make him a meat-based alternative in future. Respecting Chrissie's principles was one thing, but inflicting them upon the entire family was quite another. She reckoned Nick was already suffering quite enough, without having his diet modified by his sister's preferences.

'I s'pose you're going to do vegetables as well,' he continued in the same disgusted voice.

'Actually, I wasn't,' Fran told him. 'I tell you what, how about if I cook you a sausage and chop it up and put it in your bit?' she offered, and got a relieved grin as her reward.

'Thanks,' he said, and then looked longingly at the door. 'Can I go now?'

'Have you finished your homework?'

'Yes,' he replied without a flicker.

'All of it?'

His eyes slid away. 'I don't have to do the rest till tomorrow,' he told her, but she didn't believe a word of it.

'Well, if you do it tonight, you won't have to worry about it tomorrow, will you?' She smiled at him blandly, and with a theatrical sigh he slumped back down into his chair at the table and opened his books again.

At least he was straightforward, Fran thought to herself as she cooked his sausage. Difficult, lively and as wriggly as a fish on a hook, but straightforward.

Unlike his sister. Fran eyed the ceiling, wondering what Chrissie was doing upstairs and if she ought to go and check. Nick must have caught the direction of her gaze, and his next words caught her completely by surprise.

'Don't worry about Chrissie. She's always like this if we get someone new. She'll come round.'

Fran was relieved to hear it. Many more evenings like this, and she would be ready to strangle Chrissie, problems or no problems. She turned Nick's sausage, stirred the vegetables in the pan and added a tin of baked beans, put the topping on the pie and slid it into the oven.

No doubt Chrissie would push it round on her plate and leave it, but that was her loss. She and Xavier were having fresh trout later, when he got home, and she was already looking forward to it. Their cheese sandwich seemed a long time ago and she was hungry.

At least, that's what she told herself, and if there was rather more to her anticipation than that, she chose to ignore it.

Xavier was finding it hard to concentrate. Taking Fran out in the car had been a mistake. He'd been all too conscious of her next to him, the slim length of her thighs, the curve of her hip, the radiance of her smile.

He couldn't believe how clear her skin was, almost translucent. He wanted to touch it, to trail his fingers over the fine line of her jaw and down the slender column of her throat.

He wanted too many things, things he couldn't have, things he had no business thinking about. He needed to pay attention to what he should be thinking about—the patient in front of him.

Unfortunately there was nothing he could do for her. She wanted a cure for her chronic back pain, and he couldn't offer her a cure, because it was due to the wear and tear on her joints and he couldn't perform miracles.

He explained to her yet again what the problem was, and gave her a repeat prescription for anti-inflammatories and referred her to an osteopath. That would at least bring her some symptomatic relief and make her more comfortable.

She still wasn't happy and, because he was the way he was, he gave her another five minutes of precious surgery time, even though he was already running late. He had two more patients to see, both of them hopefully reasonably routine, but, then, so was Mrs

Jowett, and this consultation was hardly running to plan.

'Mrs Jowett, there really isn't any more that I can do for you today,' he explained patiently. 'What I suggest we do is you go and see the osteopath, take the anti-inflammatories and I'll see you again in a fortnight to review your progress. If it isn't beginning to improve, then I can refer you to the hospital pain clinic, and if you run into real difficulties in the meantime, please, come back. OK?'

That seemed to satisfy her. The promise of the pain clinic, like a carrot dangling in front of her, led her out of the door at last and Xavier was able to deal with his final two patients and get home.

He was ridiculously eager, like a schoolboy with a crush, and as he turned onto his drive he forced himself to pause a moment. Hands on the wheel of his stationary car, he took a few steadying breaths and gave himself a stern talking-to.

'She's not for you. That's not why she's here. Remember why she's here—for Chrissie, and for Nick.'

He repeated it like a mantra as he walked into the house—remember why she's here, remember why she's here—but the moment he caught sight of Fran in the kitchen and she turned and smiled at him with that wonderful smile, he forgot.

'Hi,' she said softly, and his heart turned over in his chest.

'Hi,' he echoed, just as softly. He shrugged out of his jacket and hung it on the back of the door, having to restrain himself almost forcibly from taking her in his arms and greeting her with a kiss. 'Sorry I'm late,' he said. 'I had a patient with a chronic pain problem, and I couldn't hurry her.'

'It doesn't matter, I've only just got the kids sorted out.'

'Problems?'

She shrugged slightly. 'Not really problems...' She hesitated, obviously unwilling to say too much, and he guessed that Chrissie had been giving her the run-around.

'She'll get used to you,' he said, hoping it was true, but Fran just smiled.

'That's what Nick said. He told me she's always like this with a new person. Is that right? And have there been many?'

He dropped into a chair at the table, ran his hand through his hair and sighed. 'Unfortunately, yes. We've had childminders, an au pair who was hope-less, and a housekeeper who bullied them. It's been a disaster, really, what with one thing or another. But she'll come round, she's a good kid really.'

He almost felt like crossing his fingers under the edge of the table. Instead, he went to the fridge and took out the bottle of Chablis that had been gently chilling all afternoon. He held it up to Fran, one eye-brow raised in enquiry, and she smiled and nodded.

'What a good idea,' she said softly.

He got two glasses down out of the cupboard and thought how oddly comforting it was to reach for two and not for one. Somehow drinking alone seemed like a weakness, where sharing a bottle of wine with a friend was a social event.

He pulled the cork, poured the glasses and slid one along the worktop to Fran. She turned from the stove, raised the glass to him and smiled.

'Cheers,' she said, and he lifted his glass and clinked it gently against hers.

'Cheers,' he repeated.

Their eyes locked, and after an endless moment she looked away and returned her attention to the stove, and Xavier retreated to his chair at the table and struggled for sanity.

Fat chance. She was bending over to check the progress of the trout under the grill, and he was treated to taut denim over a firm, rounded bottom that made his body ache.

So much for sanity!

# CHAPTER FOUR

FRAN spent the next few days settling in. The following day, Friday, she managed to get the children to school at a reasonable time so that she wasn't late for work. Chrissie continued to be obstructive, but Fran just worked round her and made no more concessions than she would have done for anybody else.

Nick, of course, was just Nick, sweet and sunny and disorganised, and so like her own brother that she just dealt with him automatically. He was also her life-saver, because Chrissie used a sort of shorthand on her palm and Nick had to translate.

Of course it would have been too much to ask Chrissie to write it out in full in longhand. Anyway, there wasn't time for the great Mexican standoff just before school, so she made do with her translator and vowed to deal with the situation over the weekend. She'd get a list of short forms from Xavier, and learn them.

And then it was the weekend, and she didn't really know what she was supposed to do. She was in the awkward situation of being neither a member of the family nor a guest and, although her flat was lovely, there wasn't a great deal to do in it.

She took herself off into town on Saturday and bought some food, just a few store-cupboard items so that if she wasn't supposed to be eating with them, she would have something to cook for herself.

Then she wandered up and down the Thoroughfare,

feeling a little lost. Apart from Jackie, she'd lost touch with most of the people from up here since her parents had moved away, and she wasn't sure where any of them might be.

Apart from Louise, of course. She knew where she'd find her—at her stable yard, up to her neck in horses, if she wasn't at a horse show. With nothing better to do, she went back to her car and drove over to Louise's.

She found her friend in the tack room, leaning back in a chair with her muddy, booted feet propped up on a scruffy table, a paper full of greasy chips open on her lap.

With a cry of welcome she catapulted to her feet, throwing the chips on the table and scattering them everywhere, and hugged Fran enthusiastically.

'It's so good to see you! I thought you'd died or something. Where've you been? Fancy a coffee? Sit down—there isn't anywhere clean, you'll just have to make do. How are you?'

Fran laughed and sat down, ignoring the dirt. 'I'm fine. I've been in London, and my parents have moved away, but I'm back now, at least for a while. And, yes, I'd love a coffee, thanks.' She stole a chip. 'So, how are you? Still here, I see.'

Louise smiled. 'Where else? And I'm fine, we're all fine.'

'All?'

'Yeah, me and Freddie and the baby. You did know I'd had a baby, didn't you?'

'A baby? No, I didn't know you'd had a baby. How lovely!'

So, while Louise made coffee and Fran ate her chips, Louise told her all about her new family, and then she plonked the coffee down in front of Fran and said, 'So what brings you back to this neck of the woods? I thought you were settled in London?'

'Long story. Anyway, I've got a job up here now, working as a practice nurse in the mornings and housekeeping for the GP and his kids in the afternoons. His daughter's disabled—'

'Not Chrissie?' Louise sat bolt upright, her face alive with interest, and Fran nodded.

'Yes, that's right. Why, do you know her?'

'She used to ride here—until the accident. How is she? Tell me all about her.'

For a moment Fran hesitated, wondering about patient confidentiality, but it wasn't really an issue. Chrissie wasn't one of her patients and, besides, she knew that anything she told Louise wouldn't go any further.

'She's in a wheelchair, and she doesn't talk.'

'I know,' Louise said, 'but I'd heard there wasn't anything wrong with her, that it's all psychological. Is that right?'

Fran nodded. 'So her father tells me. Nobody seems to know why, exactly—obviously it's something to do with the accident, but she won't talk about it, apparently. She's just locked up in there.'

'That's really sad.' Louise shook her head and buried her nose in her coffee for a moment. Then she looked up and put her head on one side thoughtfully. 'How about RDA?'

'Riding for the disabled?'

'Well, she always loved riding. Her parents had talked about getting her a pony, but her father was a bit reluctant. You know what doctors are like—he was worried about the danger, I suppose. You could ask him about it—about the RDA. I run a group here—actually, her favourite pony is one of my best. Maybe she could join the group.'

'Could she ride him? That pony?'

'She—and, yes, she could. Her name's Misty.' Louise leant forward, eyes alight with challenge. 'I tell you what, why don't you just bring Chrissie down here one day and I'll conveniently have the pony tied up in the yard? Then we could mention the RDA, and if she's interested, maybe we could take it from there.'

It was an idea, and one that teased at the back of Fran's mind for the rest of the weekend. She was too busy, though, to really give it very much consideration, because on Sunday Xavier asked her if she had anything planned.

'I'd like to take the kids out and the dogs, and go for a walk. I thought we could go up to Ickworth House—there are flat paths there, and an adventure playground where Nick can let off steam for a while, and we could have lunch in the restaurant. I thought you might like to come.'

And so they went to the stately home, almost like a real family, and she and Xavier strolled side by side while he pushed the wheelchair through the park, and Nick ran backwards and forwards with the dogs on their leads and squandered some of his abundant energy.

Fran would have liked to have gone into the house, but she was sure that it would go down like a lead balloon with the children and, anyway, the dogs wouldn't have been allowed.

Instead, they went up to the adventure playground

and Chrissie sat in her chair and watched wistfully as Nick climbed around the apparatus.

'Fancy a swing?' Xavier asked her, and Chrissie gave a noncommittal shrug. He turned to Fran with a slightly strained smile. 'Could you hang on to the dogs for me for a moment, please?' he said, handing her their leads. Lifting Chrissie easily out of the wheelchair, he carried her over to the swings and set her gently down on a seat.

'You'll have to hold your legs up a bit,' Fran heard him tell his daughter, and she wondered if he was doing it for Chrissie's enjoyment, or as a form of physio to make her move her legs.

Whatever, it seemed to work, because she lifted her legs out of the way so that her feet didn't scrape on the ground, and he pushed her, gently at first and then higher, until her eyes were alight and her hair was flying.

Fran stood by the wheelchair, holding the dogs and keeping an eye on Nick, and then finally the swing was slowing and Xavier carried his daughter back to her chair, a healthy glow in her cheeks and a sparkle in her eyes that Fran had never seen.

She ought to be running, Fran thought, flying along with the wind in her hair—or riding.

Maybe she would drive her by Louise's, and let her see the pony. It wouldn't do any harm, and if it sparked an interest that might lead to her recovery, so much the better.

It had been a lovely day. Xavier stretched out on the chesterfield in his study, the dogs at his feet, and wondered what it was about the day that had been so special.

Fran. An image of her leapt to mind, her wide smile, the sparkle in her eyes, the way she scraped back her hair and tucked it into a hairband to stop it blowing around. Lifting her arms like that had pulled her sweater taut over her firm, full breasts and he'd had to look away before he'd disgraced himself.

Even so, the image had stayed with him for the rest of the afternoon, tormenting the life out of him.

It had been fun to talk to her on the way back as well, while Nick played with his GameBoy and Chrissie stared out of the window. Just talking to another adult about nothing in particular assumed enormous importance when you were a single parent, he'd discovered, and Fran was easy to talk to.

She was upstairs now, pottering in her flat, and he didn't know whether to leave her alone or invite her down to share a glass of wine with him. He could always give her the option, of course, he told himself, and headed for the kitchen.

He tapped on the door at the bottom of the stairs and opened it a crack. 'Fran?'

She appeared almost instantly at the top of the stairs, her smile welcoming. 'Hi. Come up.'

He hesitated for a second. He hadn't been in the flat since she'd moved in, because he didn't want to invade her space, but need and curiosity got the better of him and he had to force himself to walk and not run up the stairs. He'd just like to see what she'd done with it—how homely she'd made it.

'I wondered what you were doing,' he said by way of explanation. 'I thought, if you were at a loose end, you might like to join me for a glass of wine.'

She smiled, and his heart jerked against his ribs and he realised just how close he was standing to her on the tiny landing. He leant back against the wall and raised an eyebrow enquiringly. 'So?'

Fran shrugged. 'I've just made coffee. Why don't you join me for a change?'

'Are you sure I'm not intruding?'

Her laugh rippled through him, teasing his nerve endings to attention.

'Of course you're not intruding. I'm not doing anything. There's nothing decent on the television tonight, so I was just going to read a book. Come on through.'

It was lovely in her little sitting room. He realised he'd never sat in there before, and suddenly it seemed an oversight. Maybe, though, it was only lovely because Fran was there, too, because there was nothing personal in the room at all to speak of. She seemed to travel very light—no physical baggage at all, just emotional.

Not as much as him, though. Nobody had as much emotional baggage as him, he thought wearily.

Xavier drank the coffee she gave him—instant, and a bit too milky, but curiously welcome—and they talked yet again about nothing very much.

Then she tipped her head on one side and looked at him searchingly. 'About Chrissie,' she said, and his heart sank.

'What about her?'

'She looked so happy on the swing today. You couldn't see her face, but she was really enjoying it. I just wondered...I know that she likes ponies, and I wondered if you'd thought of her going to the RDA.'

He shook his head hastily. 'We went once—I thought it might help her. It was an absolute disaster.

The children all had head injuries, and she hated it. She wouldn't even get on. We had to leave.'

'Maybe it was just the wrong group?' Fran suggested. 'Maybe on a more individual basis—'

He shook his head again, remembering the look on Chrissie's face. 'No. There's no point, Fran, it won't help. Nothing will help.'

He felt the defeat rising up to swamp him again and, setting his cup down, he got to his feet.

'I'll go now, I'm not very good company,' he said to her tiredly. 'I think I'll have a hot bath and an early night. Thanks for the coffee.'

He went through the door onto the main landing, checked that the children were both asleep and went downstairs. The dogs were waiting hopefully for him in the kitchen, and he put them out in the garden for a run, then gave them a biscuit in their beds before pouring himself a small brandy and taking it upstairs.

It was only ten o'clock, but it felt much later. He went into his bedroom and closed the door, stripping off his shirt as he went through to his bathroom and turned on the taps.

A long, hot soak would do him the world of good, he told himself, and he wouldn't even think about Chrissie and how little he could do to help her...

If Fran had thought that the weekend would have mellowed Chrissie towards her, she was mistaken. On Monday morning, she was as obstructive and awkward as possible, and Fran remembered that she still hadn't got the shorthand sorted out.

She decided to deal with it that evening, and then remembered that she had to take Chrissie to physio after school that day. Actually, she realised, that would provide her with a perfect opportunity to sit down with Nick and get him to give her a comprehensive list of all the abbreviations that Chrissie used, while his sister was being treated.

'Right, Chrissie, it's time to go to school now,' she said, her fingers crossed behind her back, but Chrissie simply ignored her. 'Have you got all your books?'

Again, the young girl ignored her, and Fran gritted her teeth and turned to Nick. 'Are you ready?' she asked him, and he nodded.

'Chrissie's ready, too. She's just being awkward.'

Chrissie shot him a black look but Fran ignored it. There wasn't time to get involved in complicated arguments, she'd worry about it later.

'Right, then, let's go.'

She grabbed the car keys, flicked the brake off the wheelchair and propelled Chrissie towards the door without waiting for any further protest. Nick trailed behind, managing to let the dogs out, and by the time Fran had rounded them up and chased them back inside, she knew she was bound to be late.

Oh, well, she was only on a week's trial. If Xavier found her too impossible, he could always get rid of her, she thought in resignation. Just at that moment, she really didn't care. The thought of continuing to do battle with Chrissie for however long it took was less than appealing.

The alternative, however, was possibly even less appealing, and by the time she got to school, she'd got a bit of stiffness back in her spine. She wasn't going to let a sulky teenage girl get the better of her, and, anyway, there was Nick.

She loved Nick. She knew exactly where he was coming from, and if it wasn't for the fact that he would have been disgusted, she would have hugged him.

She waved goodbye, and watched Nick push Chrissie towards the school entrance before jumping back in the car and driving quickly to the surgery.

This time she was ten minutes late, and it threw her out for the rest of the morning. Angie brought her a coffee when she had finished her own surgery, and out of the kindness of her heart she took some of the notes of the remaining patients and dealt with them herself.

Fran hated it. She hated not being able to do everything easily and without thinking, she hated not knowing where anything was, or what the local protocol was for all the procedures.

She just felt like a misfit, and it was only when she was walking through the waiting room after she had finally finished and saw Xavier waiting for her that her spirits lifted.

'Hi, there,' he said with a smile. 'All done?'

She nodded. 'Finally. I owe Angie one,' she told him. 'I ran over, and she took some of my patients.'

He studied her thoughtfully for a moment, and then checked his watch. 'I don't have any calls, and I've got an hour before I have to be back. Why don't we go to the pub and have some lunch and chill out a bit?'

Fran gave a bitter little laugh. 'Because I don't deserve it?'

'Nonsense, of course you do. Starting a new job is always a nightmare. There's nothing worse than settling in. You'll be fine, don't worry. How was Chrissie this morning?'

She stifled a little snort. It was her problem, and

she really shouldn't make it his. Not if she wanted to keep her job, anyway. 'I'll cope,' she said economically, intending to let it go at that, but Xavier had other ideas.

He ushered her out to the car park, and settled her in the front seat of his sports car while she did her best to preserve her dignity in a dress that seemed determined to ride up. 'She doesn't hate you, you know. She hates herself,' he said almost absently as they drove off.

Could he read her mind? Apparently. She shot him a wry smile. 'I know that. She's just testing me. We'll get through it, given enough time.' She settled back into the comfortable leather seat and changed the subject adroitly. 'So where are we going?' she asked him.

'Just a quiet little pub in a village near here. They do good, cheap lunches, the service is quick and the view's nice. It'll cheer you up.'

Fran didn't like the thought that he felt she needed cheering up, but he was probably right, she admitted to herself wryly, and, anyway, she wasn't going to pass up the opportunity of having lunch with him. He was good company, she was starving hungry and, provided they stayed off the subject of Chrissie, they should be fine.

They ate their sandwiches in the garden, because it was so mild, and they hardly spoke at all. They didn't need to. Just being in each other's company seemed to be enough.

For Fran, who talked almost constantly, it made a refreshing change. Perhaps Xavier and his children were exactly what she needed to unwind the tightly coiled spring inside her heart.

They went back to the surgery, and she went home,

threw a casserole together for supper and went and collected the children.

'Chrissie's got physio,' Nick said, dithering from foot to foot, 'and Pete's mum said I can go home with him for tea, so is that OK?'

'Would your father let you do it?' she asked him, and he nodded.

'I do it all the time.'

Fran looked at Chrissie. 'Is that right, Chrissie?' she asked her, but Chrissie just shrugged.

No help there, then.

'Where is Pete's mother?' Fran asked Nick, and he ran off, returning a moment later with a smiling middle-aged woman with a youngster of Nick's age in tow.

'Are you sure this is all right?' Fran asked her. 'Nick says he does it all the time.'

Pete's mother nodded. 'Yes, he does. They practically live in each other's pockets.'

Satisfied that Nick would be returned to them later, Fran allowed him to go and then had to deal with the problem of getting Chrissie to the physio without directions. She had a fair idea of where it was, but Chrissie's obdurate silence didn't help.

For the second time that day, she was late because of Chrissie, and she decided she would have to do something about it. The physio was ready for them, and Fran sat down and flicked through a magazine for half an hour and wondered how on earth she could get through to the girl.

Maybe this was an opportunity to take Chrissie on her own to Louise's—always assuming, of course, that Louise was there.

She'd put her number into the memory of her mobile phone, and she slipped outside for a minute and rang her friend.

'I know it's probably a nightmare time to suggest this, when you're feeding the horses and bringing them in and trying to get home to your baby, but is Misty anywhere near the yard at the moment? It's just that I've got Chrissie on her own—'

'Brilliant! Misty's right here, so now would be fantastic. Shall I put the kettle on?'

'No, don't do that. I'll just park the car next to the yard and come and find you in the tack room.'

'Tap the horn as you drive in. I'll grab Misty and casually walk past. See you soon.'

Fran put her phone away and went back inside, just as Chrissie wheeled herself back into the waiting room.

'All set?'

'I can't make Thursday afternoon,' the physio told Fran, 'so could you bring her on Friday at lunchtime? About one?'

'Sure,' Fran said with a smile. 'How did it go?'

The physio looked surprised that Fran had even asked. 'Oh, OK. No change, really.'

Fran nodded. It was only what she'd expected. The physiotherapy was simply holding Chrissie's body in an uneasy status quo and preventing it from deteriorating. However, such a holding pattern could only last for so long, and then irreversible damage would have taken place.

Fran had to get her on her feet again, sulky and bad-tempered or not—her professional pride simply wouldn't allow her to do anything else. So she was a trauma nurse. So what? This child was traumatised, both physically and mentally, and she thought it was a very good job that Misty didn't know just how much she was relying on her to help!

'I just want to pop in and see an old friend,' Fran said over her shoulder to Chrissie as she turned on to the road that led to Louise's yard. 'You don't mind, do you?'

She didn't expect a reply, and she wasn't disappointed. That was fine. She didn't need an argument about this, particularly not with somebody who wouldn't argue back. However, as they drove down the road she did watch Chrissie's face in the rear-view mirror, and it went utterly still.

Good, she thought. A reaction.

She tooted the horn as she drove down the track, and a moment later Louise appeared around the end of the barn, a grey pony in tow. Fran pulled up beside the yard and got out, giving Louise a hug.

'Hi!' she said, as if she hadn't seen her friend for ages. 'It's good to see you again. I thought I'd pop in and sort out something for tomorrow night.'

Louise looked past her, and smiled and waved. 'Is that Chrissie in the car?'

Fran turned casually back to the car and nodded. 'Yes. Do you know her?'

'Of course I know her. Hi, Chrissie!'

They walked round to the side of the car, and Fran slid open the wide side door, opening the whole side of the car so that Misty could stick her head inside.

Automatically, Chrissie's hands came up to stroke her, and as Misty nuzzled her and chewed her blazer button, Chrissie even laughed. Her arms came up and circled Misty's neck, and she buried her face in Misty's mane and clung on.

Misty was a star. She didn't try and pull away, she

just stood there and allowed Chrissie to cuddle her for ages while Louise and Fran made arrangements to meet the following evening as their cover story.

Finally, Louise turned to Chrissie. 'So, how are you? It's good to see you again. Misty's missed you. You ought to come up and ride her some time.'

Chrissie disentangled herself from the pony and looked up at Louise hopefully.

'Would you like that?' Louise asked her, and Chrissie nodded, excitement shining in her eyes. Louise turned to Fran. 'We'll sort something out tomorrow night,' she promised. 'I'm sorry, I have to dash, I've got to get home to the baby. I'll see you soon, Chrissie,' Louise said.

She towed Misty out of the car, and Fran slid the door shut, casting a despairing glance over Chrissie's uniform as she did so. It was going to take a bit of sorting out to clean it up before tomorrow, she thought, but, judging by the look on Chrissie's face, it was worth it.

All she had to do now was run it past Xavier and get his agreement.

# CHAPTER FIVE

FRAN was hoping to have a chance to talk to Xavier that night about the riding, but in the event she decided it wouldn't be wise.

He came home in a foul mood, and immediately asked her where Nick was.

'He's at Peter's,' she began, and he turned to her, his brows dragged together in a scowl.

'Why?' he asked, his voice very quiet and controlled.

'He asked if he could,' she explained. 'I spoke to Peter's mother, and she seemed quite happy. She said they often do it.'

'They do,' he told her curtly, 'but never on a school night. He's not allowed to go out on a school night, and he knows that. Why didn't you ask Chrissie?'

'I did ask Chrissie,' she said. 'She just shrugged. Anyway, I didn't feel it was Chrissie's decision to make—'

'And I don't feel it was your decision,' Xavier said flatly. 'How's he supposed to get home?'

'Peter's mother's bringing him after they've eaten.'

Xavier's mouth tightened, but he didn't say any more, just helped himself to a glass of juice from the fridge and stalked off without another word.

'So that's you told,' Fran said quietly to herself. So much for their camaraderie at lunchtime, the companionable silence. Well, it wasn't companionable now. She'd thought Chrissie's silence was icy, but it wasn't a patch on Xavier's.

She checked the chicken casserole, glad that somebody had finally thought to share with her the fact that Chrissie ate chicken, and peeled the carrots with savage intensity, smart retorts and witty put downs flooding into her mind now that the conversation was over.

Technically, she thought, now that Xavier was home she was off duty. Fine. She'd dish up their supper, and take her own up to her flat and eat alone. She didn't see the point of sitting through a meal in tortured silence.

The decision made, she sliced the carrots, hurled them into a pan with little chunks of broccoli and cauliflower, poured boiling water over them and slapped them onto the hob. She was mad enough to spit tacks, and if Xavier had walked into the kitchen at that moment...well, it was just a good job he didn't.

Fran prodded the jacket potatoes in the oven, decided they were done and dished up. By the time she'd done that, the vegetables were cooked, and she drained them and put them on the plates, set two of them on the table and picked her own up. She stuck her head around the kitchen door and called the others, then stalked off up the stairs with her supper in her hand.

She didn't care whether they'd heard or not, and if they didn't get there quickly, the dogs would probably have it. Serve them right.

The casserole was done to perfection, Xavier noticed absently. Chrissie ate with more than her usual enthusiasm, but he found his appetite had deserted him.

Why had he bitten Fran's head off? She wasn't to know that Nick wasn't allowed out on a weekday, and it was Nick's fault, really, for not telling her that. He'd skin him alive later, but in the meantime, there was somebody else right under his nose who was hardly blameless.

'Why did you let Fran think that Nick was allowed out on a Monday night?' he asked Chrissie, but she just looked innocent. She was very good at that. He gave an inward sigh and gave up. Fran had obviously taken herself off upstairs in a fit of pique, and he would have to go and apologise to her shortly—if she hadn't packed and left by now.

It wasn't her fault, of course, but he'd come home in a bad mood. One of his more gutsy and charismatic patients had had a return of the cancer that they'd thought was beaten, and this time the big C looked likely to win. His role now had come down to symptom control, and that frustrated the hell out of him.

Still, he should have known better than to take it out on Fran, although as a fellow health professional she would probably understand when he explained.

He hoped.

'So, how was your physio?' he asked Chrissie.

She shrugged and waggled her thumb from side to side.

'Only so-so?'

What else had he expected? He went back to his casserole, prodding about among the chicken and mushrooms with no real enthusiasm, and then gave up. It seemed a shame to waste it, but the dogs didn't seem to mind. They just had a second helping of supper.

After Chrissie had wheeled herself off with a yoghurt and a teaspoon to finish her meal in front of the television, Xavier snagged a bottle of horribly expensive wine from the fridge, grabbed two glasses and headed for the back stairs with his peace offering.

Fran heard the knock, and for a moment she contemplated ignoring it. Then she heaved a sigh and stood up, opening the sitting-room door to find Xavier hovering on the bottom step with a bottle of wine in one hand and a couple of glasses in the other.

'Fran, I'm sorry,' he said quietly. 'I was unreasonable earlier. Can we talk?'

To her disgust, she folded like a wet tissue.

'Sure. Come on up.' She went back into the sitting room, scooping the magazine off the sofa and retreating to the single chair. Then she waited for him to break the silence.

He pulled a corkscrew out of his pocket, opened the bottle, splashed a couple of inches into each glass and handed her one.

'Here—with my apologies. Truce?'

For a moment she hesitated, then she took the glass. 'Truce,' she said quietly.

She didn't want to fight with him—it was quite hard enough, fighting with Chrissie all the time.

He dropped into one corner of the sofa, facing her, and with a sigh he looked up and met her eyes.

'About what I said earlier—about it not being your decision. That was ridiculous. Of course it was your decision to make, you're in charge of the children when I'm not around, *in loco parentis*, and you must do whatever you think fit. You don't need to refer to me for every last moment of their lives. That's one of the main reasons for employing somebody so reliable—you take some of the responsibility off me, or you would if I let you.'

He looked away, staring sightlessly across the room, and she sensed that he hadn't finished speaking. She waited quietly, and after a moment he spoke again.

'I had a patient this afternoon,' he told her, his voice curiously flat. 'She's got cancer. She's been treated, and she was doing really well, but it's come back. I'm going to lose her, and I hate that.'

Fran's animosity went out of the window at a stroke.

'Oh, Xavier, I'm sorry,' she said softly. 'That must be awful.'

He nodded. 'It's just down to palliative care now, and I know that's vitally important, but it's the part of my job that I find the hardest. I hate losing patients, especially when they're gutsy and sparky and they've already gone through so bloody much. It just seems too unfair.'

He fell silent, staring broodingly into his wine, swirling the pale liquid around the glass as if the answer lay in its depths, but there was no answer there or, at least, not one that would change anything.

Fran ached for him. She knew just how he felt. She'd felt that way so many times, when someone they'd struggled to save had died sometimes even weeks later from their injuries.

Except, of course, she hadn't really known them, whereas Xavier knew this woman, had dealt with her probably for years, and was intimately involved with her and maybe her family, her husband, possibly even her parents.

Who said general practice wasn't stressful? It was just a different kind of stress. Of course, most of the time it was much less cutting edge, but she guessed that when the tragedies happened, they were probably more deeply felt than in her old job.

Would she cope better with that sort of stress?

More to the point, would she even get a chance to find out? She hadn't been at all pleased with her performance this morning, and part of her had wondered if that was why Xavier had been short with her this evening.

In case that had been part of it, she apologised yet again for having been so late, but he dismissed it.

'Believe me, Fran, I know just what you're dealing with in the mornings. It isn't easy, especially when they aren't co-operative.'

'I just feel I'm letting Angie down.'

'Nonsense. She's been struggling without any help at all for months, and she's really glad to have you. It'll get easier, I promise, and if you get stuck, you'll just have to ask. Don't worry about interrupting her, she won't mind, and I don't mind if you interrupt me either. In fact, I'd rather you did than struggle on alone. There will be times when you need to refer a patient to me or to their own GP, and I'd much rather you were too quick to ask for a second opinion than brushed something aside.

'Now, drink up and have another glass of wine,' he said with a fleeting smile, and because it was so nice, and because she wanted to heal the breach, she agreed.

He reached across the table and poured her wine,

then set the bottle down on the table and curled his hand around the back of his neck, rolling up his head and wincing.

'Stiff neck?' she asked, but he shook his head.

'Stiff everything,' he said with a wry smile. 'My neck, my shoulders—it's just tension. I get all screwed up about things and my shoulders climb up into my ears. I just need to relax.'

He gave a tiny huff of laughter, then sighed and leant back into the corner of the sofa, resting his head. A moment later, though, his hand came up absently to run the back of his neck again, and Fran stood up, taking the glass of wine out of his hand and putting it down, then pulling him to his feet.

She hooked out one of the chairs at her dining table, and pointed to it.

'Sit down on that, and fold your arms and rest them on the table,' she instructed, and then she stood behind him and cupped her hands over his shoulders, kneading the muscles firmly.

He gave a quiet groan and dropped his head back against her, his eyes closed, and after a few moments she felt the tension ease away. She carried on until the muscles were soft and pliable, and then she paused.

He was motionless, his head resting against her, his eyes still closed. She bent over and murmured, 'Still awake?' His eyes opened and he turned towards her slightly, so that their faces were scant inches apart.

'Just about,' he said softly. 'Thank you, Fran. I don't deserve you.'

She snorted and straightened up. 'I don't know about that. I'm late for everything, I'm engaged in a battle of wills with your daughter and I'm going to make your other practice nurse so mad she's going to leave. You're probably right. You probably don't deserve me.'

Xavier laughed softly and stood up, tucking the chair back under the table and returning to the sofa. He picked up his wine, propped his feet on the table and settled his head back with a sigh.

'Deserve you or not, that feels really good,' he said, and she gave up arguing, curled up in the chair with her feet tucked under her bottom and smiled.

'We aim to please. I'm sorry I stalked off at suppertime.'

He gave a low grunt of laughter.

'It's nothing I wouldn't have done, in your position. Let's just forget it. There was something I wanted to ask you, by the way. Well, two somethings, actually. One is whether you would cover me, if I pay you more, so that I can do some shifts for the deputising service that we use.'

'Sure. And you don't have to pay me more,' she protested, but he just laughed at her.

'Wait until you hear the hours I'm talking about, and then say I don't need to pay you,' he advised.

'Whatever. I don't have anywhere else to be, so it's no problem. Just give me a few days' notice if you can.'

'I can give you weeks of notice, once I've agreed to the shifts I'm going to do.'

'That's fine, then. What was the other thing?'

He looked suddenly slightly awkward, almost shy, she would have thought if she hadn't known better.

'It's my birthday on Friday,' he told her. 'My in-laws asked me what I wanted, and I said the weekend.' He gave her a wry smile.

'So, this weekend there are no kids, and I've been wondering what on earth to do with the time. Don't get me wrong, there's tons I can do, but if you're not doing anything on Saturday evening, I wondered if you'd care to join me. The local cinema does a special deal, dinner in their restaurant and a film, but somehow going out for dinner and to see a film on your own—well, let's just say I don't fancy it, but if you're busy, just say so.'

Fran shook her head, really pleased by his invitation. 'It's my own birthday on Saturday,' she told him, 'so that would be lovely. We can both commiserate about getting older.'

He laughed. 'Well, you can commiserate with me, because I'm going to be thirty-seven, but you can't be anything like that, and if you're under thirty, I'm certainly not going to commiserate!'

'Sorry,' she said with a smug smile. 'I'm only going to be twenty-seven.'

'Just a baby,' he said in disgust. 'I might even withdraw my invitation on the strength of that.'

But there was a smile lurking in the back of his eyes, and she didn't believe him for a moment.

Just then the dogs barked, and he glanced at his watch and got to his feet. 'That'll be Nick,' he said. 'I'd better go and thank Peter's mother.'

Fran waved the wine bottle at him. 'Here, this is yours.'

He shook his head. 'Stick it in your fridge—we'll finish it tomorrow night.'

'I can't tomorrow,' she said, remembering Louise. 'I'm going out for supper with a friend—if that's OK? About eight o'clock?'

'Oh. Yes, of course, that's fine, you're free to do

whatever you like in your time off,' he said, then, excusing himself, he ran down the stairs and shut the door at the bottom just a tiny bit firmly.

Fran stared after him, slightly puzzled. He'd sounded a little—what? Cross? Curt?

Disappointed?

Surely not. She must have imagined it.

Fran felt rather more comfortable at work the following day, more familiar with the needs of her patients. As well as the routine inoculations and a dressing or two to change, Xavier rang through to her to ask her if she could look at a child who seemed to have something in her eye.

'You've probably done rather more of this sort of thing than me recently, and I don't want to have to send her to A and E if I don't have to. Do you mind?'

'No, sure, of course not.'

She went into Xavier's consulting room and found a little girl sitting on her mother's lap, struggling to rub her eye while her mother held her arm down. She crouched down in front of the little girl and smiled at them both. 'Hi, there. I'm Fran—I'm a nurse. Now, I know it's sore, sweetheart, but can you let me have a little look? There's a good girl.'

While her mother held her hands down, Fran eased the child's eyelid up and then released it immediately.

'Yes, she's got a tiny splinter in there. It must be very sore. I'll need a little spatula to get it out—have we got anything like a spud?'

Xavier nodded. 'I'll get you one. Is there anything else you need?'

'Swabs, saline, fluorescein to see if there's any

damage to the cornea, an eye patch, antibiotic eye ointment—'

Xavier threw up his hands and laughed. 'OK, all of this stuff is in your room, so why don't we just go in there?'

So they all trooped into her treatment room, laid the little girl down on the couch and Fran used the little rounded spatula, or spud, to scrape the splinter away from her eye. The fluorescein showed no further damage to the cornea, so Fran squirted eye ointment into it, covered it with a soft pad and then sat the little girl up again.

'All better now?'

The child nodded, and Fran watched her go, happy that she'd been of some use. Not, of course, that she was no use to her other patients, but this was something that she had been able to do better than anybody else in the surgery and, no matter how slightly, it bolstered her confidence.

A little later on, she was called upon to suture a cut in a farm worker's finger, something that was absolutely second nature to her, although she hadn't treated many farmers in central London, of course.

'You'll need a tetanus booster, I expect, won't you?' she asked him, but he shook his head.

'I had one earlier in the year, when I cut my other hand. Bit of a hazardous business, farming,' he said with a smile. 'Mind you, the doctor who sewed me up then wasn't nearly as pretty. It's almost worth doing it this time!'

Fran laughed at him, taped up his finger and sent him on his way with instructions to keep an eye on it for infection, and get a prescription for antibiotics if necessary.

He was her last patient, and she glanced up at her watch and did a mild double take. She had finished, and almost on time—and not only that, she'd arrived before nine. Amazing. Chrissie had been extraordinarily co-operative this morning, and Fran wondered if it was anything to do with having seen Misty.

She still hadn't spoken to Xavier about the riding, and she reminded herself that she really must do it. Maybe at lunchtime, she told herself, but he didn't come home for lunch because he had too many visits to make and he ran out of time.

And then, when she picked Chrissie up after school, she was amazed to find that Chrissie wanted to 'talk' to her.

She scribbled furiously on her palm computer and held it up for Fran to read, but Fran just shook her head in exasperation.

'Chrissie, I can't understand all the short forms you use. Can't you write it out in longhand on a piece of paper?'

Chrissie shook her head, and turned again to her palm, writing the words out in full. Then she handed it to Fran.

'"Don't tell Dad about the riding",' Fran read aloud. She looked up at Chrissie, her brows drawn together in puzzlement. 'Why not tell him? Won't he be pleased?'

Chrissie nodded, but took the palm back and wrote on it, 'I want to surprise him.'

Fran hesitated, torn between the need to get Chrissie moving and the need to get her father's permission, but then she remembered what he'd said last night about her being *in loco parentis* and to do as she saw fit, and she shrugged.

'OK,' she agreed reluctantly, 'I won't tell him, but you must.'

'Only when I know I can do it,' Chrissie replied laboriously. 'Promise you won't tell him first.'

Again Fran hesitated, then she nodded slowly. 'All right. I promise. But I don't like it, Chrissie. As soon as we know if you can manage it, you must tell him. Promise me that.'

Chrissie nodded and stuck her thumb up in an OK, and Fran let it go. 'I'll sort out a time with Louise tonight, all right?' she said, and Chrissie nodded again, her eyes shining.

'Now, how about some homework?' Fran suggested while she was winning, and without a word Chrissie got out her books and started work.

So far, so good, Fran thought. If nothing else, at least she seemed to have secured Chrissie's co-operation for a while.

That night at Louise's, she arranged to take Chrissie for her first riding lesson on Wednesday afternoon, after her swimming lesson. At any other time, she would have to find some way of losing Nick for an hour or so, and she didn't think it was fair to involve Nick in the secret. But on Wednesdays there was a standing arrangement for Nick to stay on at school, and so there would be no need to involve him at all.

That sorted, she spent the rest of the evening chatting to Louise and Freddie and cuddling their delightful little baby boy Thomas, who was eight months old and utterly delicious.

Fran went home feeling broody and lonely, and wondered if she would ever know the happiness that Louise had found.

*    *    *

On Wednesday, after Fran had taken Chrissie swimming, they went to the stables and found Misty all tacked up, ready and waiting. Chrissie changed into a pair of old jeans, and then Fran wheeled her over to the mounting block.

'Now, Chrissie, I don't think we can lift you up there, sweetheart,' Louise said. 'Misty will stand still so, if we help you, can you try and walk up the mounting block and help us get you on?'

Fran stood there in silence, with her fingers crossed behind her back, and waited to see what Chrissie would do. Would her need to get onto the pony overcome this first hurdle?

The pause seemed endless, but finally, with a steadying breath, Chrissie checked her hat, tightened the strap and shuffled to the edge of her seat. Her teeth were gritted, her face determined, and as Louise and Fran tucked an arm under each of Chrissie's and lifted her, she took the three unsteady steps to the top of the mounting block and leant, gasping, over Misty's back.

'Well done,' Louise said calmly. 'Now, when you've got your breath back, we'll give you a hand to get on.'

Fran had to hand it to her. She didn't make a great thing about Chrissie walking up the mounting block, just accepted it, and a moment later Chrissie was in the saddle, her feet automatically finding the stirrups as she picked up the reins.

'Right, hang on tight,' Louise said. 'We'll go in the sand school and I'll just lead you round for a few minutes.'

While Fran stood and watched, Louise walked

round and round and Chrissie smiled until her cheeks must have ached. All too soon, Louise brought the lesson to a halt. Although it had only been a very few minutes, Chrissie was exhausted.

They had to lift her down, and Fran realised then that, although Chrissie might not have had a physical problem to start with, the fact that she hadn't walked for the last two years had in itself created one. The immobility had taken a huge toll on her, and getting her back on her feet again was going to be a long, slow process.

However, at least now it seemed as if the process might have been started and, exhausted though she was, Chrissie's eyes were shining and she had colour in her cheeks and she looked healthy and happy and normal.

Fran could have cried with relief. Instead, she just grinned at her, gave her a brief hug and took her into the tack room to change back into her school trousers before they picked up Nick.

Two in one, she thought as they drove home. Chrissie trying to walk and actually using her legs again, and a morning in the surgery when things had gone her way and she'd felt like a valid and useful member of the team.

Maybe things were looking up at last.

The glow of that whole successful day stayed with Fran for the rest of the evening, and all of the following morning until midway through her surgery.

And then, just because it was all going so well and she didn't get that lucky, something happened to challenge her fragile confidence again.

She was in the middle of setting a patient up for

an ECG when there was a sudden commotion outside the door and she heard urgent voices and running feet.

Throwing open the door, she saw a man lying collapsed on the floor, the other patients clustered round him and a woman kneeling, crying, by his head. Without thinking, she knelt down beside him and tried to find a heartbeat, but there was none.

Oh, lord, she thought. Now what? What do I do?

Her palms started to sweat, and she could feel her heart pounding in her throat. Help, she wanted to cry. Somebody help...

And then Xavier was there, clearing the crowd, taking over from her.

'Can we have a bit of room here, please?' he said, and then he was beside her, his hands busy ripping open the man's shirt. He thumped him once firmly in the middle of the chest, then checked his pulse in his neck again and shook his head.

'Fran, get the crash trolley,' he rapped out, and she stared at him blankly.

'Where...?'

'In Angie's room—hurry!'

She hurried, on legs that shook like jelly, and found the crash trolley in Angie's room under a cover. Then she wheeled it back to him, and he charged up the portable defibrillator, slapped the paddles on the man's chest and shocked him.

'Anything?' he asked her, and she pressed her trembling fingers to the man's neck and nodded.

'Yes. He's got an output.'

Just then the man's eyes fluttered open and he groaned, and she heard Xavier sigh quietly with relief.

'OK, Mr Davies, you're all right. You've just collapsed in the surgery. Let's get you off to hospital.

Sue, can you call an ambulance?' he said to the receptionist, who was hovering nearby.

'I've done it. They're on their way. Mrs Davies, why don't you sit down here?' She put her arm round the shocked woman and helped her into a chair, and Fran brought pillows and a blanket and helped Xavier prop their patient up and set up the oxygen.

They moved some portable screens around Mr Davies, giving him a little privacy, and within half an hour he was gone, the equipment was cleared away and everything had gone back to normal.

Everything, that was, except for Fran, who was feeling sick with reaction. She went back to finish her ECG, her hands still trembling all that time later, and it was lunchtime before the shaking stopped.

Xavier found her in the kitchen when he came home for lunch, and he eyed her in concern.

'Are you OK now?'

She nodded. 'Yes, I'm fine. I'm sorry, I just froze.'

'Is that like it was in A and E?'

She nodded again. 'Yes. Lord, I feel so useless. What would I have done if you hadn't been there?'

He shrugged. 'Probably coped. Who knows? It doesn't matter. I was there, so was Stuart, and Angie wasn't far away. It wasn't your responsibility, Fran. Don't worry about it.'

But she did, of course. She worried about it all that afternoon, and all through the evening while the children were busy making birthday cards for their father, and that night, as she'd known she would, she had the dream again.

So much blood.

Bodies everywhere, people screaming for help, and nothing she could do to save them. She had blood all over her, blood from several different people, and they were all dying and she couldn't get to them in time...

She sat bolt upright in bed, harsh sobs tearing at her throat, and her arms were red from scrubbing at them in her sleep, trying to get the blood off.

'Idiot,' she told herself. 'It's just a dream.'

She put the light on and got out of bed, fighting back the tears, and went into her little kitchen and put the kettle on. She'd make a warm drink and watch television for a little while, and then maybe she'd get back to sleep again.

Or maybe not.

She reached for a mug with shaking hands, but it slipped through her fingers and smashed into the sink, and she folded up on the floor and wept silently.

'Oh, Fran.'

She felt the warmth of Xavier's body as he sat down on the floor beside her, one arm slung round her shoulders, drawing her against his side, and when the tears hiccuped to a halt she found a tissue pressed into her hands.

'Here. Mop up and have a drink. Tea, coffee, or do you want to finish that wine?'

She gave a shaky laugh. 'Not the wine. I'm making a big enough fool of myself without help,' she told him drily, and he chuckled and helped her to her feet.

'Hot chocolate?'

'I haven't got any.'

'We have, downstairs. Come on, we'll go and get ourselves a little midnight feast and keep the dogs company for a while. They'll think it's great. They like parties in the middle of the night. After Sara died we did it a lot. I think they miss my little sorties to the kitchen—and anyway, it's my birthday. We have to celebrate.'

His smile was teasing and gentle, and she dragged in a good, deep breath and let it go on a shaky smile.

'A midnight feast sounds good,' she said, suddenly realising that she hadn't eaten since breakfast. 'And happy birthday, by the way.' She followed him down the stairs, and in response to his gentle urging over their hot chocolate, she told him about her dream.

'It's being so useless,' she concluded. 'Everybody dying and I can't help. That's the worst bit.'

'Of course. That's the main stress of the job—that's what we're here for, and if we can't do it, we've failed. Of course it's stressful. I understand, Fran. I have dreams like that. Everyone does. You're not alone.'

'But it's not just in my dreams. I can't do the job in the daytime, either,' she pointed out.

'That job—at the moment.'

'Maybe not ever.'

'So? It doesn't matter. The job you're doing is no less valid for not being on the front line. Stop beating yourself up over this, Fran. You're a good nurse. You were wonderful with little Claire and her eye, and I gather you stitched Mike Barns up after he cut himself again—I saw him on the way out and he said you're prettier than me. I was gutted.'

She laughed, as she was meant to, and Xavier's mouth lifted in an answering smile.

'OK now?' he murmured, and she nodded.

'Yes,' she said, and she realised it was true, at least for the moment. She was calm again, and she knew she'd sleep.

They went up the back stairs, and on the landing she paused.

'Xavier, I'm sorry I woke you,' she said softly. 'Thank you for being so understanding—and thanks for the midnight feast.'

The smile crinkled his eyes at the corners. 'Any time,' he said. Their eyes met, and for a moment she had the strangest feeling that he was about to kiss her, but then he stepped back, and with a murmured 'Goodnight' he opened the connecting door and went through it, leaving her alone.

Not quite alone, though. She felt curiously as if he were still with her, his presence guarding her. Maybe it was just knowing he was only a few steps away through the door, or maybe it was knowing he, too, had dreams like hers.

Whatever the reason, strangely comforted, she went back to bed and snuggled under the soft, thick quilt and closed her eyes. She'd left the landing light on as usual, but she didn't need it. She slept soundly and dreamlessly until dawn, and then in that shadowy time between sleep and wakefulness she dreamed of him, and woke with the memory of his kiss still lingering on her lips...

# CHAPTER SIX

'MORNING.'

Fran looked up from the sandwiches she was making and smiled at Xavier. 'Good morning—and happy birthday again. Sleep well?'

His mouth twitched into a smile. 'Very—apart from a small excursion to the kitchen for a midnight feast. You?'

'Oh, I slept fine,' she said, her smile growing wry, 'apart from the odd nightmare and a small excursion to the kitchen for a midnight feast. Here—your birthday card. It's on the table.'

'Thank you.' He opened it and chuckled, then came over to her, standing beside her and looking down into her eyes searchingly, the card in his hand.

'Are you OK now?' he asked her, and she nodded.

'I'm fine. Thank you. I'm sorry I trashed your night.'

He reached for a packet of breakfast cereal and tipped it up over a bowl, shaking out a huge heap. 'You didn't trash my night,' he corrected her mildly. 'If anything, you made it more interesting. My nights are awfully boring these days.'

Was it her imagination, or did the words hang in the air between them? Whatever, the moment of speculation was soon gone, because Nick came dawdling into the kitchen, still in his pyjamas, and asked Fran if she'd seen his trousers.

'I expect they're on the bathroom floor, where you

left them—and can you tell Chrissie to hurry up, please? We're going to be late again if you don't get a wiggle on.'

Xavier dropped into a chair at the kitchen table, dug his spoon into his cereal and grinned at her. 'See? You're getting the hang of it already.' He munched the spoonful, and then looked up at her again. 'Are you very busy this morning? I've got some minor surgery to do, and Angie normally helps me, but she's had to go to the dentist. Do you think you could give me a hand later?'

Fran's curiosity was aroused. 'Yes, sure, if it doesn't clash with my patients. So what are you doing?'

'Removing a mole that's looking a little suspicious, removing a sebaceous cyst that's causing problems and sorting out an ingrowing toenail. Nothing exciting, I'm afraid.'

'It beats CPR hands down,' she said with a laugh that was only slightly strained. Putting the last sandwich into its bag, she went to the door to call the children and found Chrissie just getting into her wheelchair from the stairlift at the bottom of the stairs.

'Ready for breakfast?' she asked, and Chrissie nodded. 'Nick?' she called up the stairs, and she was rewarded by the sound of running feet. Ten seconds later, Nick was skidding into the kitchen in his socks, tie stuffed into his pocket, shirt hanging out and his hair quite definitely not combed.

Fran opened her mouth to comment, but Xavier got there first.

'Right. Go back upstairs, get properly dressed,

comb your hair, put on your shoes and come back,' he said drily.

With an exaggerated sigh, Nick turned on his heel and went back upstairs. Xavier shot Fran a wink over Chrissie's head and stood up, putting his bowl into the sink.

'Right, Fran, I'm off to work. I'll see if I can shuffle our patients around so we can do this minor surgery. I'll see you there later.'

He bent over and kissed Chrissie on her cheek, patted her shoulder and left the room. Fran looked at her and smiled. 'OK?'

Chrissie nodded, but she pulled a face and pointed to her legs.

'Sore?' Fran asked quietly, and Chrissie nodded again, but smilingly.

Fran was pleased. If her legs ached, it was a sign that she'd used the muscles, and that was all to the good. 'Don't forget you've got physio today at one,' Fran reminded her. I'll pick you up at a quarter to.'

Chrissie nodded, finished her breakfast and wheeled herself off to get ready. Fran glanced at her watch again and frowned. Nick was really pushing it today, she thought, but that was eleven-year-old boys for you. Well, he was going to be eating his breakfast in the car at this rate, unless she got really tough and made him go without.

Unlikely. She made him a jam sandwich, put it into his lunchbox with the rest of his things, let the dogs into the garden for one last run and put on her coat.

By the time the dogs were back inside Nick had appeared, looking puzzled.

'Where's my breakfast?' he asked indignantly.

Fran just handed him his lunchbox in silence, and

he opened it, sighed and picked up his schoolbag. 'OK, I'm ready,' he said heavily.

Suppressing a smile, Fran followed him out to the car.

'You seem to be getting on better with Chrissie today,' Xavier said when he saw Fran at the surgery later.

They were just setting up the treatment room for his minor surgery, after he'd managed by a miracle to get through his own patients on time.

'I think Nick and Chrissie have swapped places, actually,' Fran said with a chuckle. 'Ah, well, you win some, you lose some.'

He laughed, pleased to hear that she sounded as though she was coping with his often awkward and fractious children. 'How were your patients this morning?'

'Not too bad. I think I might be getting the hang of it—working without the adrenaline rush. Maybe that's what comes of overdosing on it.'

'You'll be fine. Right, I think we might be ready for our mole,' he said, looking around him at the carefully laid-out equipment. 'All set?'

Fran nodded. 'I'm ready when you are.'

She made a very good assistant. Xavier was able to concentrate on what he was doing, knowing that she would provide him with the right instrument at the right time. He realised, of course, that most of the procedures he was going to carry out that morning would have been well within her own capabilities as a nurse in Accident and Emergency, and he wondered how she must feel, being relegated to the sidelines. Maybe, though, it was exactly what she needed at the moment. She was only young. There was plenty of time for her to get back into the front line as and when she was ready.

He realised with a slight shock that that would mean her leaving them, and it was a curiously unpalatable thought.

He dropped the excised tissue into the specimen pot and sutured the resulting wound, carefully drawing the edges together to minimise scarring. He wouldn't think about Fran leaving. She'd only arrived just a little over a week ago. It occurred to him that she'd had her week's trial, and they still hadn't discussed her continuing employment.

Still, now wasn't the time. He'd discuss it with her over the weekend—just in case she was about to bottle out! He wanted to have plenty of time to reason with her, not just slot her into the three-second gap between patients.

He straightened up and flexed his shoulders, looking down at his patient with a smile. 'Right, Annabel, the result should come back from cytology in a few days, and we'll ring and you let you know the result, but I'm pretty sure you don't need to worry.'

Fran taped a dressing over the stitches and steadied their patient as she helped her off the couch.

'Are you OK there?' she asked, smiling at the young woman as she stood up.

'Just a bit wobbly,' Annabel replied with a similarly wobbly smile. 'Maybe I shouldn't have watched you do it. I'll be OK in a minute.'

'Come on,' Fran said reassuringly, tucking her arm around her, 'let's get you out of here into the fresh air, and perhaps you could have a cup of tea. I'll get someone to make you one.'

She was back in a few moments, by which time Xavier had cleared away the debris from the first operation and was scrubbing for the second.

'Do you want me to get Mr Grady in and give him his local?' Fran asked him.

'Yes, please, if you could. Then you could scrub, ready to assist me. This one might be a little trickier because it's quite a deep cyst, but it's been causing him a problem over many years apparently. Not exactly exciting, I'm afraid, but I'm sure it'll make a great difference to him.'

'Are we going to be done by twelve thirty?' Fran asked him, glancing at the clock. 'Chrissie has to be at physio at one, because it was changed from Thursday.'

'We should be, and even if we're not, I'll just finish off without you.'

They were finished in time, however, and as they were clearing up he discussed with her the arrangements for that evening.

'I'm going to run them over to their grandparents' as soon as I've finished surgery, so when you get the kids back after school, do you think you could make sure that they've packed everything they'll need? Nick, particularly, because he's so dozy he'll forget his own head one day.'

Fran laughed and patted his arm reassuringly. 'Don't worry, Xavier, I'll get him organised,' she said with a grin, 'even if it kills me.'

He watched her go, curiously comforted to know that she was shouldering some of his responsibility. He hadn't realised just how much strain he'd been under, trying to juggle their lives and make a success of parenthood, until some of that strain had been removed.

Please, God, let her want to stay. That would be the best birthday present he could have.

Which reminded him...

Fran hadn't bought Xavier a birthday present because she'd felt it wasn't appropriate, but after she'd dropped Chrissie back at school after her physio, she went into town and had a look around. She wanted something silly, something teasing and light-hearted rather than a serious gift, but as she trawled up and down the shops, she realised how little she knew about him.

What were his hobbies and interests? She had absolutely no idea. He didn't seem to have time for any, and that seemed a shame. She tried to remember what she'd seen in his study that might give her a clue, but there was nothing. Well, only books, and maybe that was the answer.

She wandered into a little bookshop that had a coffee-shop at the back, and she bought herself a cup of coffee and browsed through the books. Finally, she found a funny one about dogs, just a silly, light-hearted little piece of nonsense, and she decided it would be ideal. She bought it and headed home, with just enough time to wrap it before she had to fetch the children from school.

Nick, of course, was every bit as awkward and disorganised as she could have expected. He was excited about his weekend away with his grandparents, and pinning him down to focus on the task of packing was a nightmare. Chrissie, of course, was organisation itself, but there were things she needed help with, and

Fran was conscious of the fact that she hadn't even cooked them supper yet.

She surrendered to the lure of junk food and offered them pizza, and they fell on it like starving dogs. So much for her usual culinary efforts, she thought with wry humility as she watched them eat it. Ah, well, she was a nurse, not a cook. She couldn't do everything.

'Right, are you all packed?' she asked them, expecting a negative, but Chrissie nodded and Nick just ran off towards the stairs, reappearing a moment later with a victorious smile and his bag. There was a sleeve hanging out of the zip but, judging by the bulging sides, he was at least taking plenty.

Plenty of what, though?

'Have you got socks?'

He nodded.

'Pants? Clean shirt? Jumper? Trousers in case you do anything smart? Decent shoes?'

He was nodding like one of those dogs in the back of a car, until she got to the wash things.

'Um...'

'Go on,' she prodded. 'Toothbrush, toothpaste, flannel—'

'I know, I know!' He ran off back up the stairs again, and was only just back down in the hall with the last things forced into his bag as his father walked in through the front door.

'All set?' he asked, and Nick, still sitting on the bottom step with the zipper tab in his hand, said, 'Of course!' with all the indignation only an eleven-year-old could muster.

Fran suppressed her laugh. 'Chrissie's ready, too,' she told him, and he flashed her a grateful smile.

'OK, kids, give me ten minutes and we'll go.'

He ran upstairs, reappearing five minutes later with Chrissie's bag in his hand and wearing jeans and a jumper that made him look altogether too appealing.

Minutes later, they were gone, and Fran set about preparing a suitable birthday meal for Xavier. He'd told her he would be about an hour and a half so, allowing two hours, that would mean eating at about eight-thirty. On the other hand, if he met a lot of heavy Friday night traffic, he could be later, so she'd planned a nice creamy chicken Stroganoff and wild rice.

The Stroganoff would keep, and she'd cook the rice when he arrived back. The salad was a cheat one out of a bag and ready to go. All she had to do was make the dressing.

An hour later everything was ready, and she debated laying the table in the dining room, but that all seemed ridiculously formal for the two of them on a Friday night when they normally ate in the kitchen.

As a special concession, she got one of the old wax household candles out of the kitchen drawer in the corner and stuck it in a cup in the middle of the table.

There. Nothing too over the top that might give him the wrong idea, she thought, and then wondered just what she meant by the wrong idea.

She was being silly. He was her boss, and just because he'd been nice to her last night didn't mean he was going to follow through on her stupid dream and kiss her, however much she might want him to!

Sara's parents were delighted to see their grandchildren, and welcomed them with open arms. Of course, the children hadn't stayed there without him since

Sara had died, and he wondered if having the children on their own might turn out to be a rather different kettle of fish. They would probably be just as eager to get rid of them on Sunday night as they were to welcome them now, Xavier thought drily as he drove home.

He flexed his shoulders and savoured the luxury of the next few days. The whole weekend, and nothing to do. Well, apart from taking Fran out tomorrow night, he thought, and realised that he was looking forward to it in a way that he hadn't looked forward to anything for a long time. Maybe even since before Sara had died.

Odd, how he couldn't really even remember her now. She'd been dead a little over two years, and when he saw her face, it was in the photograph on the dresser or a clip from a video, not a real memory. Strange, how someone who had been so important to him had become just a distant mirage.

He wondered if he ought to feel guilty about it, but decided it was all part of the healing process. Maybe it had been meeting Fran that had triggered it, but certainly, since she'd arrived in his life, he'd started thinking again about things that had been buried in his subconscious for so long that he'd almost forgotten they existed.

Things like the scent of shampoo on a woman's hair, the feel of bare, soft skin against his, the warmth of a body curled against him in sleep.

Oddly enough, it wasn't his sex life that he missed so much as the things that went with it—the companionship, the sharing, not being alone at night.

'You sad old fool,' he said scathingly, 'you sound like a whining, mangy dog.'

He turned the radio on—loud, to drown out his runaway thoughts—but when he turned onto the drive at five past eight, his heart skittered with anticipation.

Ridiculous, Xavier told himself. Fran's an employee. You're being stupid. You're far too old for her, too much emotional baggage, too much baggage altogether. She wouldn't spare you a second glance, even if you had the emotional reserves or the time to take on a relationship.

Curiously depressed by that thought, he got out of the car and walked towards the door, just as Fran opened it.

She was standing in the doorway with the porch light shining on her, and her smile lit his heart.

'You're early,' she said softly, and her voice trailed tiny fingers over his nerve endings. Desire slammed through him, stealing his breath for a moment, and he paused on the bottom step and looked up at her while he gathered his composure.

'Does that mean I don't get supper?'

'No, it just means you have to wait a little while for the rice to cook.'

'I expect I can manage that,' he said with what he hoped was a normal smile, and followed her in, trying his damnedest not to stare at her bottom neatly encased in taut, faded denim. She was wearing a jumper with her jeans, a short one that hugged her waist and showed off her breasts to the detriment of his common sense.

'How about a glass of wine while you cook the rice?' he suggested, and then spent the next couple of minutes standing at the worktop, removing the cork and pouring the wine while he got his body back in order.

He hadn't felt like this since he was a teenager, and he just hoped he didn't make a complete idiot of himself before the evening was finished. He slid a glass of wine along the worktop to Fran, and then retreated with the other one to the far side of the table and safety.

It was then that he noticed the present sitting in his usual place at the table, and the old scruffy candle that he used on the drawer runners to make them slide properly, standing up in a cup in the middle of the table.

'Are you a closet romantic?' he asked her, unable to hide his smile, and to his amazement she blushed.

'Well, it's your birthday, and you aren't having a cake, so I thought you ought to have at least one candle. I would have got thirty-seven, but I didn't want to set fire to the house,' she teased, and he didn't bother to try and hide the smile any more.

In fact, he was feeling a little choked that she had actually cared enough to make the effort.

Of course, Sara would have laid the table in the dining room with crystal and silver and their best bone china, but Fran wasn't like that, and he realised that this impromptu little candle was more touching than all that pomp and ceremony could ever have been.

He fingered the present, staring at it thoughtfully, and Fran sat down opposite him and gestured towards it.

'Go on, open it, it's nothing much.'

He started by peeling the tape off it carefully, but then grew impatient and ripped the paper away. A book. A funny book, one he'd flicked through in the bookshop and which had made him smile. He'd nearly bought it for Fran, but in the end he'd gone for something much more traditional, not a book at all but flowers, a hand-tied bouquet with water in the bottom of it, which was sitting at that moment in the garage, keeping cool.

Too romantic? Possibly, but hopefully she wouldn't misinterpret his intentions—or, maybe, interpret them accurately.

He looked up at her expectant face and smiled fleetingly.

'Thank you, Fran,' he said, and his voice sounded a little gruff.

'I didn't know what to get you,' she confessed. 'I hope it's OK. I know you like dogs.'

He looked down at the dogs at his feet and raised an eyebrow. 'I like dogs?' he said to them, and their tails wagged in unison.

Fran chuckled. 'Well, they think you do.'

'Poor, deluded fools.' He raised his glass of wine to Fran and smiled. 'Thank you. You didn't need to get me anything, but it's perfect, and I appreciate it.'

Her colour rose again, and she buried her nose in her wineglass so that she didn't have to look at him.

Funny, how she could be all brash and bossy one minute, and then shy with him the next. The timer went on the oven, and she jumped to her feet with undue enthusiasm and drained the rice while he watched her masochistically, knowing nothing would ever come of it.

The meal was wonderful. To Fran's amazement and relief, the Stroganoff recipe had worked perfectly, the rice was just firm enough and the salad dressing delicious.

Xavier had three helpings, although, to be fair, the last one was just a little scraping to tidy up the bowl, and then they had ice cream—one of those hideously expensive luxury ice creams with lumps of real Belgian chocolate and a drizzle of double cream and chocolate sauce over the top.

'You could have put a candle in my ice cream,' he suggested, but she just raised an eyebrow.

'What, and have baked Alaska?'

His chuckle rippled through her, teasing her senses, and she wished she could manage to keep their relationship in perspective. However, when he was like this, it was very difficult, particularly when she was finding herself so drawn to him.

'So,' he said after a minute, 'we haven't actually discussed it yet, but I assume, since you're still here, that you're happy to stay on?'

She felt a little flicker of relief and nodded. 'Absolutely. My only problem is that I may not be able to do the job well enough for you, but if you'll keep me on, yes, I would like to stay.'

'Thank God for that,' he muttered, and lifted his glass to her. 'Here's to our new relationship. Long may it continue.'

New relationship? Had he read her mind? She lifted her glass and drained the last few sips, then pushed her chair back and headed for the kettle.

'Coffee?' she asked him over her shoulder, and he nodded.

'Thanks.'

While she made it, he cleared the table and loaded the dishwasher, then he blew out the candle and carried the coffee through to his study, the dogs trailing at their heels.

When they were settled at each end of the chesterfield, the dogs at their feet, Xavier turned to her and said, 'Have I told you just how grateful I am to have somebody to share the responsibility for the children? It's made my life so much easier this week, and I can't imagine how I managed before you came.'

He sighed and dropped his head back against the arm of the chesterfield, settling down further into the corner so that his hips were resting on the edge and his legs sprawled across the floor over the dogs.

'That's one of the hardest things about being a single parent,' he went on quietly. 'Having to carry all the responsibility, make all the decisions, deal with all the nitty-gritty every day. You're permanently on duty, and after a while it takes its toll, no matter how much you love them. But with Chrissie's problems as well, and also losing Sara so suddenly, it's just been a nightmare. Having you here now just gives me a little light at the end of the tunnel and it makes all the difference.'

Fran ached for him. She didn't say anything, because there was nothing really to say, but maybe just being there with him was enough.

For a while they were quiet, and then, quite out of the blue and without even knowing she was going to do it, she said, 'Tell me about Sara.'

Xavier turned his head towards her, looking slightly surprised, and then his eyes fell on the photograph on the wall and he sighed.

'She was twenty when we met, and I was twenty-three. It was love at first sight, or something like that, I suppose. We were very young, and not very sensible, and we got married and started a family without even thinking about how we were going to support ourselves. I was still training, I was over here without a grant and being supported by my family, and Sara was rich and spoiled and probably never imagined for a moment that her family would do anything other than continue to give her money.

'Then she discovered how wrong she was, and what it was like to be poor, and she hated it. Then an uncle of mine died and left me money, just as I qualified as a GP, and we bought this house and things started to look up. By this time we had two children, and she had a nanny part time so she was free to take up social engagements. She was a great one for social engagements.'

He sighed, obviously remembering, but he didn't look as if they were particularly happy memories.

For the first time, Fran wondered if his relationship with his beautiful, chic and elegant wife had been flawed. She'd always assumed that their marriage had been perfect, but maybe not.

'Do you miss her?' Fran asked, and he turned towards her, a strange expression on his face.

'Miss her? In a way. I miss certain things—companionship, mostly. I don't miss our social life.'

She wondered what else he might miss, but it was none of her business. She wondered if he'd had any relationships since but, again, she didn't feel it was her place to ask. None of it was any of her business, only insofar as it affected her relationship with the children, and there was no way his sex life had any bearing on their day-to-day existence whatsoever.

Or hers—something she would do very well to remember!

# CHAPTER SEVEN

XAVIER stood in the middle of the kitchen, Fran's flowers in his hands, and pondered.

Should he stand them in the middle of the kitchen table with her card propped up against them, or make her breakfast and take it and the flowers up to her flat?

Dangerous. He wasn't sure that walking into Fran's bedroom and finding her warm and rumpled with sleep was a very good idea. In fact, he'd go so far as to say that it was an extremely bad one.

On the other hand, he wanted to see her face when she got the flowers, for purely selfish reasons, but he didn't know when she was going to get up. She might lie in until lunchtime, and why shouldn't she? It was her day off. There was nothing in her contract that said she needed to get up and entertain him at the weekend, and it was only nine o'clock.

'Oh, hell.'

He put the flowers down in the middle of the kitchen table, propped his card up against them and put the kettle on. He'd make some tea, have his breakfast and just wait for a while—and if in the end he decided to be sensible and go and get on with his day and she still wasn't down here, well, tough. So he'd miss her when she found the flowers. So what?

He didn't miss her, though, because a moment later he heard the water running in her shower room overhead, and then a few minutes later she ran lightly down the stairs and into the kitchen. He was sitting on the opposite side of the table, and so he got a grandstand view of her face when she caught sight of the flowers.

It had been worth waiting for.

She ground to a halt, her mouth fell open and then slowly closed, and her eyes sparkled with tears.

'Oh, Xavier,' she said unevenly, and, reaching out a trembling hand, she touched one of the white roses with a fingertip. She looked up at him, a sudden uncertainty in her face. 'Who are they for?' she asked, as if she didn't really believe they could be for her, and he was glad then that he hadn't bought her a book or any of the other things that he'd considered.

'Well, they're not for me, and I don't see anybody else here,' he teased gently, and her eyes filled and spilled over.

She dashed the tears away with the back of her hand, and gave him an unsteady smile. 'They're lovely,' she said, and her mouth wobbled. She bit her lips and picked up the card, opening it and reading it. It made her laugh, a slightly choked laugh that broke the tension, and she looked back up at him with a smile that could have lit up the world.

He couldn't believe just how much they'd meant to her. They were only flowers, for heaven's sake. Sara would have taken them from him with a smile and a light kiss on his cheek, and that would have been the end of that. Fran couldn't take her eyes off them. She kept touching them, reaching out and fingering the wispy petals of the white spider chrysanthemums, running her fingers down the stems of the roses, gazing at them as if she'd never seen anything like them in her life.

'Happy birthday,' he murmured, and she turned to him with shining eyes.

'Thank you,' she said softly. 'Thank you so much. I can't tell you—the last time I had flowers was on my sixteenth birthday, and my father bought them for me. They're so pretty.'

Not as pretty as you, he could have said, but he managed to clamp his mouth shut before he put his foot in it. Buying her flowers for her birthday was one thing, commenting on her appearance was quite another and moved the whole thing into a different league. Even in his demented state, he could appreciate that.

'Cup of tea?' he offered, trying to get everything back onto an even keel, and she pulled herself together visibly and flashed him a smile.

'Thanks—don't get up, I'll get it. Would you like another one?'

'I'm fine.'

He was, he realised. She'd brought light and colour into his day already, and he hadn't even had breakfast yet. He sat there and sipped his tea, and watched Fran as she got down a mug and glanced at her flowers, and poured milk into the mug and glanced at her flowers—it was a good job she couldn't wear them out by looking at them or they'd be wilting already, he thought with an inward smile.

The dogs were sitting at Xavier's feet, staring devotedly up at him, and he patted their heads absently as he watched Fran. 'All right, girls, we'll go for a walk later,' he promised.

'Are you going anywhere nice?' she asked him. 'Only it's a beautiful day, and I'd thought of going for a walk somewhere pretty—by the river or something. Maybe we could go together?'

It was so long since Xavier had gone for a walk with any company other than the dogs that he'd almost forgotten what it was like. Suddenly an ordinary dog walk had turned itself into a social event, something to look forward to and anticipate.

'Why not?' he said, trying to sound casual and probably failing dismally. 'We'll have breakfast and then go, if you like.'

The dogs, as if understanding him, wagged their tails enthusiastically, and he stifled a laugh.

He could empathise with that!

It was a wonderful walk. They took the car, and drove down to the Kyson Point car park, then walked down to the river and along the river bank and up Martlesham Creek, while the dogs sniffed happily about and thoroughly enjoyed themselves.

They weren't alone in that. Fran hadn't enjoyed a walk so much for ages, partly because she'd been in London, and partly because walking on your own was never much fun and she hadn't had a lot of choice.

None of her friends and colleagues ever wanted to walk anywhere if they didn't have to, and because so much of getting around London was done on foot, the concept of going for a walk just for the fun of it was totally alien to most city dwellers.

Xavier, too, seemed to be thoroughly enjoying himself, and she wondered when he'd last had a decent walk in company. It would be hard for him to take Nick out and leave Chrissie behind, and, of course, taking Chrissie involved taking the wheelchair, and

where they were at the moment, that would be completely impossible.

They made their way back, and as they walked she
looked at the other side of the river, where the bank
shelved gently up to the tree-line, and there, right on
the edge of the trees, she caught the gleam of glass.

Looking closer, she realised that it was a house,
carefully designed to be almost invisible, and she
pointed it out to Xavier.

'I think that must be Josh Nicholson's house,' he
told her. 'It's somewhere on that side of the river,
anyway, and there's nothing else until you get right
up to Melton.'

Fran studied it with interest. Just think, if she'd
taken Josh's job, she might have been living there.
How odd. She wondered how he was, and if he'd
managed to get someone to look after him. Was he
stuck with his mother? Poor Josh.

Still, she couldn't regret the decision—especially
not today, her birthday, with those beautiful flowers
sitting on the kitchen table and the glorious sunshine
and Xavier at her side.

'It must be very peaceful over there.'

'Very isolated. It wouldn't be everybody's choice,'
he said.

'Maybe he needs it, as a retreat from the world. I
wonder what it's like to be so famous?'

'I wouldn't mind a stab at being so rich,' Xavier
said with a wry smile. 'I know I'm not exactly struggling, but it would be very freeing not to have to earn
a living and to be able to do what you truly wanted
to do instead of what was necessary.'

Fran looked at him curiously. 'So, what would you

do differently if you didn't have to worry about money ever again?'

He gave a soft laugh. 'Probably nothing. I'd still want to be a doctor—a GP. I wouldn't change the house, although I'd probably spend some money on it, because it's looking rather tired in places. What about you? What would you do differently?'

Fran shrugged. Not having to worry about money was such an alien concept she couldn't imagine what that would be like. 'I don't really know. I'd probably buy a house like yours—or Josh's, over there.'

'They're very different,' Xavier said in surprise.

'I suppose they are, but in a way they're not. They're both beautiful, yours in a very classic way, Josh's, I suppose, because of the setting as much as anything. I'd love to have a house overlooking water.'

'I'd like to have a house that didn't let it in,' Xavier said with a laugh. 'If you get a choice, I'd go for Josh's. Mine is very old in places, with all the problems that entails, whereas Josh's is very new and, I would imagine, very high-tech. Lonely, though,' he added, and there was a touch of sadness in his voice, as if loneliness was something he lived with every day.

Even if he and Sara hadn't had the world's most perfect relationship, presumably they had been happy enough, or they would have been separated. It must have been the most horrendous shock to lose her so suddenly, Fran thought, and wondered how on earth he'd coped with his world falling apart around him.

'So, go on, then, what else would you change about your life?' he asked, and she thought about it for a moment and shook her head.

'I don't know. Just at the moment I don't know

what I want anyway, so it's hard for me to say what I'd change. Let's face it, there isn't very much in my life *to* change at the moment—well, nothing permanent, anyway.'

'What about your job?' he asked, and she wasn't sure if she'd imagined it, or if there was a strange inflection in his voice.

'I'm quite happy with my job,' she replied honestly, and realised that it was true. Her early teething troubles at the practice seemed to be over, and she was making huge strides with Chrissie. Nick, of course, was just Nick, bless his heart, and then there was Xavier.

'No, I wouldn't change my job,' she said firmly, just so that he was sure.

'What about going back to A and E?'

She shook her head emphatically. 'No. Not now, anyway, and probably not ever.'

'You may change your mind,' he said softly. 'I wouldn't want you to feel trapped with us if you do. I can always get somebody else.'

Somebody else? Did that mean he didn't really want her? She felt suddenly racked with doubt, unsure of the security that she had maybe begun to take for granted a little too soon.

No. She was being silly. He'd told her only last night how pleased he was to have her there, so that he could hand over the responsibility for the children to her for part of the time. She was just being paranoid now, she told herself, and put her doubts firmly aside.

It was her birthday, and she was having a lovely

time, and she wasn't going to allow anything to spoil it—particularly not when it was probably a figment of her imagination.

Fran didn't know how much she should dress up for their date that evening. She stood in front of the wardrobe, flicking through the hangers dispiritedly.

Nothing. She had nothing to wear, nothing but jeans and evening dresses and an interview suit that probably didn't fit her any more.

Unless, of course, she wore her little black dress. That was probably too small as well, but she might just get away with it, and at least it was totally uncontroversial. She took it off the hanger and wriggled into it, eyeing herself critically in the mirror, and decided it would have to do.

It was a little snug over the bust, but if she didn't eat too much she might get away with the waist. At least it wasn't frilly or glittery like some of her other evening stuff, and it was a huge improvement on her jeans!

She took it off and put it back on the hanger, then showered and put her make-up and underwear on before shimmying back into the dress. She did the zip up as far as she could, then slipped on her shoes, picked up her coat and bag and went down into the kitchen.

Xavier was in there, looking quite mind-blowingly gorgeous in a dark suit and tie, his shirt startlingly white against his slightly olive skin. He ran his eyes over her appreciatively, and she felt suddenly shy.

'Could you do my zip up for me, please?' she asked him a little warily, hoping it didn't look staged, but he just said, 'Sure.' She turned her back to him and tried not to think too much about the touch of his fingers against the nape of her neck.

Then it was done, and he was moving away, leaving the scent of his aftershave drifting on the air around her. It was clean and citrusy, and she inhaled slowly before turning round and picking up her coat again.

'Well, I'm ready,' she said brightly, looking up at him, but he seemed to be avoiding her eyes, unless she was imagining it. She seemed to be imagining rather a lot of things at the moment, so it wouldn't surprise her.

With a tiny inward sigh, Fran followed him out of the door, slid into the passenger seat of his sports car with as much dignity as she could muster, and while he was walking round the back to his door, she tugged the hem of her skirt down.

She didn't know why she bothered, because he didn't give her legs a second look. He just started the car, and drove down into town in silence, parking outside the cinema and ushering her in without so much as a word.

Now what had she done wrong? With a mental shrug, she allowed the waiter to take her coat and seat her, and then, as Xavier took his seat opposite her, she met his eyes challengingly.

He returned her stare unblinkingly for a moment, then his mouth tipped in a rueful smile.

'Sorry. I was somewhere else. How about a drink while we wait?'

'I'll just have a glass of white wine, thank you,' she replied, and picked up the menu. She wondered where the 'somewhere else' was. With Sara? Maybe this had been one of their regular venues. She hoped not, but even if it was, tonight was hardly a date.

It was just two single people hooking up with each other to make a simple meal and a film a less isolating experience. Nothing more than that—even if it was her birthday.

It certainly wasn't a date.

However, as the meal went on, it began to feel more and more like one. Xavier was attentive and charming, and he talked easily about all sorts of things, and maybe it was because of that that she allowed herself to be lulled by the romance of the moment.

And then, of course, there was the film—a light-hearted romantic comedy with just enough tender sensuality to make her wish that she wasn't going to be alone tonight.

Maybe it had affected him, too, because he was quiet again on the way home, and she fully expected that when they went in, he would take himself off to his study alone and she would be dismissed.

Fran was wrong, though. He headed straight for the kitchen, picked up the kettle and held it up to her in enquiry.

'Coffee, or something stronger?'

She'd only had one glass of wine with her meal, and it was, after all, her birthday.

'Have you got any brandy? I wouldn't mind a tiny one, if you have.'

'Sure. Do you want it straight, on ice or with a mixer?' he asked, and she just smiled.

'Will you kill me if I have it on ice?' she asked him, but apart from pulling a wry face, he didn't comment, just dropped three ice cubes into a brandy glass, poured a little brandy over them and handed the glass to her.

'Here you are. As it's your birthday, I'll indulge you.'

As she'd known he would, he had his brandy straight, and when she sipped, she realised why. It was smoother than any she'd ever had, and probably horribly expensive. Still, she liked it with ice and, as he'd said, it was her birthday.

They went into the study, and for once the dogs didn't follow them, but stayed idly in their beds.

Xavier sprawled in his usual attitude on the chesterfield, tugged his tie down and undid the top button of his shirt, then turned to her and raised his glass.

'Happy birthday.'

'Thank you. And thank you for this evening. I enjoyed it.'

'What did you think of the film?' he asked her, and she smiled.

'Funny, silly—great entertainment. I liked it.'

He nodded, but he looked thoughtful again, and she wondered if he was thinking about Sara. Probably.

Fran dropped her eyes to her brandy, swirling the ice round in the pale liquid and trying not to feel jealous. Crazy, really, when the woman was dead, but that didn't necessarily diminish her hold on his heart, even though he'd said that he didn't really miss her.

Maybe this was one of those times when he did and, if so, perhaps she ought to get out of his way and leave him alone with his thoughts.

She drained the last of her brandy and stood up.

'I'll leave you in peace now,' she said with a forced little smile.

Being the gentleman he was, he got to his feet, put his brandy glass down and opened the study door.

Of course, if she hadn't stumbled over the corner of the rug, it might never have happened, but she did stumble, and he reached out to steady her and their eyes met and they froze.

'Fran?' he murmured, and then she was in his arms, and his lips were on hers, claiming them, plundering them, his hands tunnelling through her hair and anchoring her head as he ravaged her mouth with his.

He pressed her up against the desk, and she reached behind her and put down the glass before wrapping her arms around him, slipping her hands under his jacket and running her palms up his ribs and down the powerful column of his spine.

One hand left her hair and made its way downwards, his knuckles trailing over her cheek, her throat, over the swell of her breast and down, his hand turning so that his palm wrapped warmly around her hip and urged her against him.

A savage groan was dragged from his throat, and his hand slid down her thigh and up under the hem of her skirt, cupping her bottom, holding her even closer.

He muttered something in French, she had no idea what, but it sounded dark and urgent and needy.

He lifted his head a fraction and looked down into her eyes, and his own were blazing with passion.

'I want you,' he said unnecessarily, and her breath caught in her throat.

'My room or yours?' she asked without hesitation.

'Yours,' he said, his voice tight, and, releasing her, he took her hand and led her up the stairs, across the landing and through the communicating door.

He stripped off his tie, tore the buttons off his shirt in his haste to get rid of it and kicked away his shoes, then trousers and briefs and socks in one swift movement.

'I can't—the zip—' she began, but he turned her round and slipped it down, much more slowly than she thought he would have done, and then slid the dress off her shoulders and down over her hips to the floor.

He drew her back against him, his body hot against her spine, and she felt the soft whisper of his breath against her ear as he murmured something in French. She didn't know what he said, didn't understand it, but it sounded incredibly romantic and it nearly made her knees buckle.

'Fran?' he murmured, and she turned in his arms and lifted her mouth to his.

His body was trembling under her hands, his mouth urgent, searching, his hands everywhere, touching her, learning her body as he moulded it to his. They fell together onto the bed, between them dispensing with the remains of her underwear, and then their bodies were locked together, driving towards a common goal, striving for the unattainable.

She felt sweat break out on his skin, felt the hammering of his heart against her own, and then she felt the ripples start deep inside her, spreading out through her whole body until there was nothing but white light and sensation and the muffled cry of his release.

Xavier lay on his back, staring up at the ceiling, stunned.

He'd never meant to do this, had never thought for

a moment that the evening would lead him here, to Fran's bed.

Never in his wildest imaginings had he dreamt of anything as spectacularly all-consuming or earthy as their frenzied coupling. He'd never behaved like that in his life, never lost control to this extent, never needed a woman as he had needed Fran tonight.

She was lying beside him, her head on his shoulder, her arm draped across his waist, and as he lay there, he was absently running one hand up and down her spine, soothing her, reassuring her as she slept.

He thought of Sara, and how different their love-making had been. This would have terrified her, disgusted and appalled her—as it appalled him, but for totally different reasons.

He could have hurt Fran. He had been out of control, driven by an animal instinct that he hadn't known he possessed, and he felt ashamed.

She moved against him, slowly waking, and she lifted her head and looked down at him and smiled.

'Hi,' she said softly, and kissed him.

He felt tenderness well up inside him, tenderness and regret, and he took her gently into his arms and made love to her again, slowly and thoroughly, taking care not to hurt her this time, and when it was over he kissed away her tears and cradled her against his chest and wished that they could have a future together instead of just some sordid, secret little affair.

'Are you all right?' he asked her softly, and she nodded.

'I'm fine. You?'

'I'm fine,' he lied, but he wasn't, and the ache inside was for Fran and what he was going to do to her, because there was no way he had the time or emotion to spare to do a relationship justice. It simply wouldn't happen, and he wished with all his heart that he could turn the clock back to that moment in the study when she'd stumbled.

He should have let her go, should have stepped away from her, instead of kissing her and dragging her upstairs and having the most mind-blowing sex he'd ever had in his life.

Because that was all it could be, just sex, and Fran was worth more than that, far more.

He could have wept with regret.

# CHAPTER EIGHT

'WHAT'S wrong?'

Xavier turned his head towards Fran and gave her a smile which she thought was meant to reassure her. 'Nothing's wrong,' he said, but his smile was strained and didn't reach his eyes, and she knew he was lying.

She rolled onto her front and propped herself up on her elbows, looking down at him solemnly. 'Please, don't lie to me,' she said softly. 'I know something's the matter. Is it Sara?'

He shook his head. 'No, it's not Sara. It's nothing.'

His accent was more pronounced, she noticed, as it often was when something affected him. She laid her hand tenderly against his stubbled cheek and sighed. 'You regret it, don't you?' she said, and he turned away, avoiding her eyes.

Gently, she turned his face back towards her and kissed him.

'Talk to me.'

'We shouldn't have done it,' he said, his voice gruff with emotion. 'I can't offer you anything, Fran—I can't marry you, I can't even openly have an affair with you, not only because of the children but because I just don't have enough emotional energy to do a relationship justice. Not now, not until Chrissie's sorted out—if it ever happens. I'm sorry—so sorry, but there's nothing I can do about it, and it isn't your fault.'

Fran suppressed the hurt and conjured up a smile.

'I don't remember asking you to marry me,' she said in what she hoped was a teasing voice, and a fleeting smile touched his lips and was gone.

He sighed and rolled towards her, one hand coming up and cupping her cheek in a mirror image of her own gesture. 'I don't regret it for me,' he said gently. 'How could I? I just don't want you to be hurt, and I know you will be.'

'Why don't you let me worry about that?' she murmured. 'I'm a big girl, Xavier, I can make my own decisions.'

He shook his head slowly. 'I should never have done it, Fran. I should have had the self-control to stop, but I don't seem to have any self-control where you're concerned. You drive me crazy, make me behave in a way I've never behaved in my life. I've never, ever done what I did tonight—just let go like that, gone wild. I can't believe I did.'

She couldn't stop the smile. 'You should probably try it more often, then, because it certainly works.'

To her amazement he coloured and gave a startled little grunt of laughter.

His knuckles grazed her cheekbone tenderly. 'I was afraid I'd hurt you,' he confessed, and Fran chuckled.

'I think I'm a bit tougher than that,' she assured him. 'Besides, you were hardly violent.'

He shook his head in bemusement. 'I have no idea what I was,' he admitted. 'You made me crazy.'

'You made me pretty crazy, too,' she said, and, drawing his head closer, she kissed him.

'Nothing has changed, Fran,' he warned her. 'We can never have any more than this.'

'Well, we'd better make the best of it, then, hadn't we?' she murmured, and kissed him again.

*     *     *

It was only later as they were lying together in the dark, their limbs still entwined, that Fran realised that they hadn't used any form of contraception.

Rats. An unplanned baby was absolutely the last thing that either of them needed at the moment. She turned her head towards him, trying to make out his features in the dark.

'Xavier?'

He made a sleepy, contented sound and reached for her. She thought of saying something, but there was no point. She was right at the end of her cycle—there was no need to worry him unnecessarily.

He drew her into the comfort of his arms and kissed her tenderly, and she forgot her fears. Forgot everything, in fact, except the heat that flared between them almost instantly at his touch. Instead, she concentrated on the man whose gentle hands were taking her to places she'd never even dreamed of...

They spent Sunday, or part of it, in the garden, tidying up the beds ready for the winter, and then at four o'clock Xavier straightened up and sighed.

'I have to go and get the children now,' he said. 'How about a cup of tea before I leave?'

Fran nodded and pulled off her gloves. 'OK. You empty the barrow, I'll put the kettle on,' she said, and went into the kitchen. She wished he didn't have to go, that the children didn't have to come back, not because she didn't want to see the children again but because it meant the end of this special time they'd had together.

Forty-four hours, she thought, that was all, and yet it had been enough to tilt her world on its axis.

She filled the kettle and put tea bags in the pot, but before it had boiled Xavier had come in with the dogs, kicking off his boots by the back door and shrugging off his old gardening coat. He went straight to the sink and washed his hands, and as she handed him a towel, their eyes met.

The towel fell unheeded to their feet, and with a ragged sigh he drew her into his arms and cradled her against his chest.

'I don't want this to end,' he said gruffly. 'I love my kids, I'd give them the world, but this time with you has been so precious...'

He broke off, his arms tightening around her, and as she lifted her head his lips found hers and clung.

They didn't bother with the tea, they just went back up to her room and stole those last few precious minutes together before he had to leave.

Finally, he dragged himself away, and Fran went downstairs and fed the dogs and sat with them, staring at her beautiful flowers and wishing it didn't have to be like this.

Sara's parents were cooking a big meal for Xavier and the children before he brought them back, so Fran made herself an omelette and took it into his study. And while she sat there, eating it, with the dogs at her feet, she studied the photograph of Sara on the wall and wondered how she had ever imagined that she might be able to take that sophisticated woman's place.

Foolish optimism, she thought. Xavier had made it quite clear that he wasn't either able or willing to make a commitment to her. She had no idea where they would go from here. It hadn't been discussed, apart from the fact that they couldn't be seen to be having an affair because of the children, so that meant sneaking around at lunchtime, probably, at best.

At worst, this one weekend might be all that they ever had—at least, until Chrissie was sorted out. Wasn't that what he'd said? That he couldn't do their relationship justice until Chrissie was sorted out?

But if—when—Chrissie was sorted out, maybe then it would be different, she thought. She was already improving, doing more for herself, and her attitude to Fran had been transformed since her riding lesson.

Please, God, let that be the key to her recovery, for all our sakes, she thought fervently. Maybe then she and Xavier would have a chance.

It was very strange, Fran thought on Monday evening, being back to normal and yet not normal. They were all in the kitchen, Nick finishing his homework and Chrissie reading a book while Xavier sat sprawled in the chair with the dogs at his feet and leafed through one of his professional journals.

She had to cross behind him to get a saucepan from the cupboard on the other side of the room, and before she was aware of what she was doing, her hand started to lift to touch his shoulder in passing.

Instead, she tucked her hair behind her ear and wondered how long it would be before something stupid gave them away. It was incredibly hard, trying to re-establish the polite friendliness of their previous relationship after their wildly passionate weekend.

Several times that evening she caught his eye and had to turn away before her face betrayed her feelings to the children. She could remember being their age, and she knew it would be very dangerous to underestimate just how much they would notice, and how aware they would be of the undercurrents between the adults.

Then at last the children were in bed, and they took their coffee into the study and closed the door.

Xavier sighed and shook his head, sprawling into the corner of the chesterfield and regarding her steadily.

'This is a nightmare,' he said. 'I so nearly put my arms round you at the sink, and every time you looked at me...'

'I know. Still, I'm sure we can manage.'

'We have to. They mustn't know,' he said. 'Whatever happens, they mustn't find out. They've had enough to deal with, what with losing their mother and Chrissie ending up in a wheelchair. I can't disturb the status quo, and I won't. As far as they're concerned, you're just a housekeeper and childminder, nothing more.'

And what about you? she wanted to ask him. What am I to you?

But in her heart she knew, and she didn't need him to tell her. What she didn't know was what was going to happen next, but she didn't feel she could ask. Silly, really, after the closeness of their weekend, but there was a world of difference between sexual intimacy and a relationship that could be taken for granted, and she was under no illusions about which they had shared.

So she drank her coffee in silence, while Xavier stared broodingly into his mug and said nothing, and in the end she stood up and bade him a formal goodnight and went to bed.

Fran woke in the morning to a crippling stomach-

ache and the knowledge that there would be no un-
wanted child, and she sat on the loo with her arms
draped over the edge of the basin beside her and cried
her heart out.

'You're such an idiot,' she said crossly to herself,
but she was exhausted with emotion and lack of sleep,
and the tears kept coming. Finally they ground to a
halt, and she blew her nose and washed her face in
cold water and had a shower, and by the time she was
dressed and downstairs, she more or less had her composure back together again.

It didn't fool Xavier, though, and he took one look
at her and frowned slightly. He came over to the
worktop where she was making sandwiches, and under cover of getting himself another cup of tea, he
murmured, 'What is it?'

'Nothing,' she muttered. 'I feel a bit rough—that
time of the month, that's all.'

Relief flickered in his eyes and he rested a hand on
her shoulder briefly. 'I'm sorry,' he said, but she
knew he wasn't, and neither was she—not really. Not
with the part of her that was still tenuously connected
to her common sense.

He poured himself more tea and returned to the
table, organising the children.

By the time he went to the surgery, they were all
but ready, and Fran simply had to drive them to
school and make her way to the surgery for nine
o'clock.

She arrived at five to nine, and was immediately
summoned to Xavier's consulting room.

'What is it?' she asked him as she went in, but he
just stood up and came towards her.

'Close the door,' he said softly, and when she

turned back he was there, folding her in his arms and hugging her gently. 'Are you still feeling rough?' he asked, and she nodded and gave in to the luxury of being held.

'I'm sorry,' he murmured. 'But I have to say I'm relieved. I thought last night—we were irresponsible at the weekend, and it didn't even occur to me. That was unforgivable, especially under the circumstances, because with Chrissie like this I really couldn't take on the responsibility for another child. Nick's neglected enough as it is. But I'm sorry you're feeling rough.'

'Don't worry, it's fine, I'll live,' she said, easing away from him because it was just too tempting to stay there in his arms for the rest of the day.

'Go home to bed at lunchtime,' he said. 'You might feel better for a good sleep.'

Her body might, she acknowledged later, but no amount of sleep was going to alter the fact that she couldn't have a lasting relationship with the man she loved.

For the first time, Fran found herself missing the hustle and bustle of A and E. At least there, she would have been so busy she wouldn't have had time to brood on her personal life.

She inoculated two babies, changed a dressing, took umpteen blood samples and did an ECG. Nothing, really, that she couldn't have done with her eyes shut, and although it was exactly what she'd wanted, she could have done with something a little more distracting.

When her last patient had gone and she had cleared up the room, she contemplated going home as Xavier had suggested, but the empty house held no appeal.

Instead, she put on her coat and went for a stroll along the riverside. She passed the tide mill, and walked along the quayside until she came to a brick-built building that was undergoing restoration.

As she drew level with it, a man in a wheelchair was being pushed down a makeshift ramp from the doorway, and he looked up at her with those amazing blue eyes and smiled.

'Well, if it isn't the most beautiful nurse in the world,' he said, theatrically pressing his hand to his heart, and despite herself she laughed.

'Hello, Josh. How are you? Still alive, I see.'

'Oh, yes, he's still alive,' the elegant middle-aged woman behind him said drily. 'Alive and just as awkward as ever,' she added, and Fran's mouth twitched.

His mother, she imagined, and suppressed the smile.

'So what brings you out here onto this draughty quayside?' Josh asked her.

She shrugged. 'I just finished work at the surgery. I needed a bit of fresh air.'

He glanced at his watch then back to Fran. 'Fancy lunch? My mother's going to abandon me in a minute, but if you've got time I could take you somewhere nice and feed you, and talk you into taking my job.'

His eyes were twinkling, but for all that, she thought he was probably serious. For a moment she was almost tempted. No emotional hassle, no heart-break, just fun with this man with the teasing eyes and wicked grin. But then she remembered Chrissie and the riding lessons, and Nick with his boundless energy. She couldn't abandon them to someone else. And then there was Xavier—always Xavier.

'It doesn't look as though you really need me,' she

said with a smile, deliberately keeping it light, and his mother—if it was his mother—snorted quietly and rolled her eyes.

'I wouldn't be too sure of that, if I were you,' she retorted. 'We're driving each other mad, but it's nothing new. It's been the same since he was born. I'm sure we'll live, but I think you probably made the right decision. How is Dr Giraud? He's such a nice man, I always think.'

You and me both, Fran thought. 'He's fine,' she replied.

'Well, if you ever change your mind, just ring me,' Josh said, handing her his card. 'I'm sure my mother and I would both be most grateful.'

She took it, and tucked it into her coat pocket. 'I'll bear it in mind,' she promised. 'You take care of yourself, now,' she added, and as his mother wheeled him away, she stared after him thoughtfully and wondered how different her life would have been if she'd taken his job instead of Xavier's.

Who would have taken Chrissie riding? No one— and would anyone else have understood Nick as she did?

And Xavier. She thought of someone else in his arms, holding him, loving him as she had at the weekend, and pain lanced through her.

No. She had made the right decision—even if her heart was going to end up in a million pieces at the end of it...

On Wednesday afternoon, Fran took Chrissie swimming and then on to Louise's for her riding lesson. Misty was all tacked up ready and waiting, and as they helped Chrissie up the mounting block, Fran could feel her positively fizzing with excitement.

Once again, Louise led her, making sure she was safe while at the same time encouraging her to use her legs and hold them in the right position. They even tried a little trot, which made Chrissie laugh out loud, something Fran had never heard.

She dragged in a deep breath and blinked away the sudden tears that sprang to her eyes. If only Xavier could see her now, she thought, but yet again Chrissie had insisted that it should remain a secret.

'OK?' Louise said, smiling up at Chrissie, and Chrissie nodded vigorously.

They helped her off the pony and back into her chair, and Louise tied Misty up and followed them into the tack room where Chrissie was changing.

'Well, that was excellent,' she said briskly to Chrissie. 'I think next time, if you feel brave enough, you can do it off lead. What do you think?'

Chrissie's eyes were like saucers, and her smile would have lit the world.

'I think that's a yes,' Fran said with a laugh, helping her back into her school trousers. 'Same time next week?'

Louise nodded. 'Absolutely. I think it's very important to keep it going.'

She took Chrissie home, picking Nick up on the way, and while they were doing their homework at the kitchen table and Fran was preparing the supper, she kept catching Chrissie's eye.

She was still fizzing, and Fran wondered how on earth Nick could fail to notice her euphoria.

Never mind her father, when he came home, but

he was so busy avoiding Fran's eye and trying to keep his hands off her that he didn't even notice Chrissie.

So many secrets, Fran thought, and wondered what Nick could dream up to add even greater confusion. She felt hysterical laughter bubbling up inside her, and had to rummage about amongst the tins in one of the low cupboards until she got it under control.

It wasn't funny, really, she thought. She was a very open person, very upfront about everything, and she hated secrets.

Not that she would have wanted the children to know about her and Xavier, at least not yet, but she desperately wanted to tell him about Chrissie, to share the joy and excitement of watching her improve, and to let him see her happiness.

'Not yet,' was all Chrissie would say on the subject, though, and Fran had given her word.

However, not everything could be kept secret, and the following day, after Chrissie's physiotherapy session, the physio came out and spoke to Fran.

'Her legs seem much stronger,' she said, sounding surprised. 'Have you been doing anything different?'

Chrissie sent Fran frantic signals with her eyes, and Fran just shook her head slightly, very conscious of Nick's presence beside her. 'I don't know,' she said innocently. 'I've only just taken over.'

'Well, whatever you're doing, I should carry on,' the physio said. 'It's the first improvement she's made in two years.'

As they left, Fran and Chrissie shared a smile, but Fran was worried. Now she was lying to the physiotherapist, and that really rankled.

'Chrissie, we're going to have to tell him, you

know,' she said firmly when they were alone, but Chrissie was stubborn.

'Not yet' was her only comment on her palm computer, and Fran just shrugged. After all, Xavier had entrusted her with responsibility for the children, and this was positive, not negative, so she knew that in the end when he did find out, he would be pleased.

Pleased, that was, about Chrissie's progress, but whether he would be pleased about her part in it, she wasn't sure. Still, she was riding the same pony in the same place as she had before, and he'd sanctioned it then, so why not now?

When Xavier came home that night, he told her that he'd arranged his dates for the deputising service, starting the coming weekend.

'I'm doing all day Saturday, if that's OK,' he said. 'It'll mean you having to take Nick to his football match on Saturday afternoon, if you can bear it. Is that OK?'

'Football?' Fran said with a smile. 'That'll cost you extra. I remember football—I had a boyfriend once, when I was about sixteen, and I had to stand on the sidelines and cheer for hours in the rain. I vowed I would never do it again.'

'How much do you want?' he asked her, and her jaw dropped slightly.

'Don't be ridiculous, I don't want anything! It was a joke, Xavier. I don't want paying at all, you're already more than generous. I'm happy to look after the kids when you do this. It's all part of the job.'

Because they were alone, she went up on tiptoe and brushed a kiss against his cheek, and with a muffled groan he turned his head and his lips found hers.

It was the first time he'd kissed her for days, and

when he eventually lifted his head, there was a dull flush on his cheeks and his chest was rising and falling rapidly.

'How do you do that to me?' he asked, his smile unsteady. 'I only have to look at you and I want you.'

Fran was relieved to hear it. He'd been so distant, so undemonstrative all week that she'd been afraid he'd lost interest. No such thing, apparently, just keeping a safe distance in the interests of their joint sanity.

He moved away from her, busying himself with the kettle in the corner, and a second later Chrissie wheeled herself into the room, Nick hard on her heels.

He must have heard them coming, and thank goodness he had, because she didn't want to explain to the inquisitive thirteen-year-old and her even more inquisitive eleven-year-old brother why she had been standing in their father's arms!

The weekend, fortunately, was warm and dry and sunny, and the football match could have been quite a pleasant experience if it hadn't been for Chrissie. They took the dogs with them, and Chrissie sat on a rug with Fran, with Martha and Kate at her feet, and sulked throughout the entire game.

'Chrissie, I'm sorry, but I can't leave you at home,' Fran said, not unreasonably.

'Want to go riding,' Chrissie wrote on her palm. 'Hate football.'

'Well, you and me both, sweetheart, but until you tell your father, there's no way I can take you riding at the weekend anyway, is there?'

Chrissie retreated into mutinous silence—not that she was ever anything but silent, but this silence had a different quality about it and Fran could feel the animosity coming off her in waves.

She ignored the girl, watching the football match with an intensity that her boyfriend of eleven years ago would have found astonishing, and when Nick scored a goal, she yelled and clapped and whistled as loud as any of the other parents.

Not that she was a parent, of course, and she'd do well to remember it. It would be all too easy to slip into the role of mother to these two sometimes difficult but infinitely lovable children, but she hadn't been invited.

In fact, she had been specifically uninvited, she reminded herself. Hired help and bit on the side, that was her role, and she wasn't even sure about the latter. Still, no doubt all would be revealed in time.

She just wished he'd get on with it!

# CHAPTER NINE

FRAN'S fears were unfounded. On Monday morning she bumped into Xavier in the office just as she was leaving.

'I should be able to get home for lunch today,' he said, drawing her to one side. 'Will you be there?'

'Yes—do you want me to cook you something?'

His mouth quirked in a fleeting smile. 'It wasn't really lunch that I had in mind,' he murmured, and she felt a soft tide of colour sweep over her.

'I'll be there,' she promised.

He was home less than an hour later, and without hesitation he drew her into his arms for a long, mind-drugging kiss. 'I've been wanting to do that for such a long time,' he said with a sigh. 'I just daren't touch you when the children are in the house, I don't trust myself. I know what you do to me.'

He lifted his head and searched her eyes. 'I need to make love to you,' he confessed softly. 'I haven't been able to think about anything else all morning.'

'Nor have I,' she admitted with a wry smile. 'Not for days.'

His eyes darkened, and he lifted Fran effortlessly into his arms and strode up the stairs.

'You'll hurt yourself!' she protested with a startled laugh, but he just smiled and shook his head.

'I don't think so,' he replied, and carried her into her bedroom and dumped her on the middle of the bed. Without preamble or hesitation, he stripped off his clothes, knelt on the bed beside her and undressed her slowly and systematically, kissing every last inch as it was revealed.

Their love-making was wild and tender and all-consuming, and when it was over they lay in each other's arms while their hearts slowed and the moisture dried on their skin.

'You are the most amazing woman,' Xavier said to her softly, tracing a line from her chin down over the hollow of her throat to one nipple, circling it idly. 'Beautiful.'

'You've been so cagey, I thought you'd gone off me,' she admitted, but he just shook his head slowly and kissed her again.

'Not a chance,' he told her. 'You mean so much to me, Fran,' he went on, his eyes serious. 'You've transformed my life, brought colour back into it, and you're good for the kids, too. Nick's much more co-operative these days, and I don't know what you've done to Chrissie, but she's a different girl.'

She wanted to tell him, but she'd promised Chrissie, given her her word, and she couldn't go back on it.

'Maybe she's just growing up,' she offered, because it was possibly true anyway, and the closest she could get to changing the subject without being obvious. 'Anyway, I'm glad you aren't going off me.'

'Not a chance,' he repeated, and just in case she was under any misapprehensions, he showed her all over again.

From then on, they settled into a routine. When Xavier could get home at lunchtime and Fran wasn't busy with the children, they would make love in the sanctuary of her bedroom, but when the children were around, they were very careful to keep their relationship hidden.

They seemed to be quite successful at it, because the children didn't seem to notice anything untoward in their behaviour, or if they did, they didn't comment, and as they usually commented on anything out of the ordinary, Fran thought they had probably escaped detection.

Then one night she had a nightmare again, and Xavier came into her room and talked to her until she had everything back in perspective. Then, without thinking, he leant over and he kissed her goodnight, and they very nearly lost their resolve.

Reluctantly, he dragged his lips from hers and straightened up. 'I want so much to spend the night with you, to wake up with you at my side, but we just can't,' he said dispiritedly. 'Never mind, maybe the children can go to Sara's parents again for the weekend soon.'

He kissed her again, a chaste kiss this time, and left her. She didn't want him to go because she was afraid the nightmare would return, but he must have soothed her because when she dreamt this time, it was beautiful.

She was walking along a track beside the river, and it was early morning and the mist was swirling across the water, colouring everything a soft, translucent grey so that it seemed only half-seen, almost imagined.

It was breathtakingly lovely, the most beautiful place she'd ever seen, and when she woke, she felt at peace.

\*     \*     \*

The air had grown cooler now, the leaves were off the trees, and when Fran came home at the end of the morning, she would take the dogs out in the garden and they would bounce around in the fallen leaves and chase the squirrels up the trees.

She was happy, happy and settled in a way she hadn't been since her childhood, and she owed it all to Xavier.

November passed, and Chrissie's riding improved hugely. Louise didn't lead her now, and she was able to trot the obliging Misty round in the sand school on her own.

'Surely you're good enough now to tell your father,' Fran said after one lesson when it was obvious Chrissie had made great strides, but she shook her head.

'I want to be able to do a rising trot properly,' she wrote on her palm computer, and that was the close of the subject.

Well, Fran thought, she could see it was only a short time away, and so she let it go. Anyway, she had other things to worry about.

She'd had an invitation to a private view at Josh Nicholson's new gallery on the quayside. It was the opening exhibition, and she realised that it must be the building that she had seen him coming out of that time they'd met on the quay.

'Please come,' he had written on the card, and she asked Xavier if she could have the evening off.

'I've got an invitation to a private view at Josh Nicholson's new gallery,' she told him, and he smiled wryly.

'So have I,' he told her. 'Shall we go in relays, or

should I see if I can get a babysitter and we could make an evening of it?'

Fran could hardly believe her ears. It was unheard of for him to suggest that they should go out together while the children were around, because until now, apart from their one weekend, they had only had those stolen moments while the children had been at school.

This was almost a public acknowledgement that they were having a relationship, and almost certainly the children would see it as that, although, of course, they could always explain it away as being more convenient.

'Are you sure?' she asked, wondering if he'd really thought about it, but it seemed he had.

He nodded slowly. 'Yes, I'm sure,' he said, and her heart soared.

Did this mean that he was getting ready to go public?

Possibly, but Fran wasn't going to allow herself to read too much into it. However, she decided it justified a new dress, and she went into Woodbridge on the first Saturday in December and found one to replace her old 'little black dress' which was rather tired now. It had a low scooped neckline and tiny spaghetti straps, and it was very elegant.

Expensive, but elegant, and it would last her for ages.

Anyway, she didn't care. If Xavier liked it, then it would be worth it, she reasoned, however much it cost.

The private view was the following Friday, but on Tuesday afternoon Xavier had a call from Josh's mother to say that she was worried about him.

He rang Fran at home while she was cooking supper and told her that he might be late, and when he came in he told her why.

'He's got a pin track infection, nothing drastic but just enough to make him feel really rough. He needs to rest, but with the gallery opening on Friday, I don't see it happening. I'm going to drop him in a prescription later,' Xavier went on. 'I forgot to take a new prescription pad with me in my bag, and I'd run out, so I'm going to have to go back there—unless, of course, you fancy doing it for me?' he added with a smile, and Fran just laughed.

'You're just trying to get out of having to go back there,' she teased, but he shook his head.

'I thought you might like to see it,' he said. 'It is a wonderful house. You could see what you've missed—although that's probably a bad idea. Maybe I'd better take it.'

Fran laughed. 'Not a chance,' she replied. 'I'll take it.'

When they had finished their supper, Xavier gave her directions to Josh's house, and as she turned onto the track and headed along the edge of the river on the opposite side to Woodbridge, the mist started to curl across the water.

It was so like her dream, except that it was night-time now and in her dream it had been morning, but even so the similarity was startling.

The track turned left and came to stop in front of the house, and the security lights came on, illuminating a broad sweep of lawn leading down towards the veiled water. She went up to the front door and rang the bell, and after a moment it was opened to reveal Josh standing there in a pair of boxer shorts and nothing else, apart from the metalwork holding his leg together and the crutch he was leaning on.

She could see the livid network of scars across his abdomen and chest, including the fine line by his shoulder where she had sewn him up in London all those weeks ago.

'Don't tell me, I look like Humpty Dumpty,' he said drily, and she laughed.

'No, you're much thinner than him,' she teased, and she stepped into the hall and looked around.

It was a beautiful house, solid pale oak floor and doors, wonderful pictures on the walls and a tremendous feeling of space and light. It was lovely, but not as homely as Xavier's Georgian house with its scarred old oak kitchen and the dogs lying around in heaps.

She handed him the prescription, including a couple of pills to start him off which Xavier had had in his bag, and then tutted.

'You look awful, you should be in bed,' she chided gently.

'I was,' he pointed out. 'I had to get up to let you in.'

He turned and hobbled away from her, and she followed him down the corridor to a huge, airy bedroom which she imagined must overlook the river. The bed was rumpled, and automatically she straightened the sheet, plumped the pillows and fluffed the quilt up.

'I knew it, you're aching to look after me,' he teased her as he sank down onto the bed and groaned.

'In your dreams,' she replied. 'I should imagine you're a nightmare to look after. Here, let me tuck this pillow in beside your foot to keep the weight off it.'

Fran brought him a fresh glass of water from the

kitchen, gave him the first pill and then, having satisfied herself that he would be all right, she let herself out.

It was wonderful there by the river, with the woodland at her back, and she stood for a moment and listened to the silence. Little rustlings, and the sound of the wind in the trees, and the mist swirling over the water—it was unbelievable, and she could have been living here.

Without Xavier, of course, and that was unimaginable. With one last look at the mist on the river, she got into her car and drove back to him.

'How do I look?'

Fran twirled in the kitchen, basking in the warm glow of appreciation in Xavier's eyes, deliberately fishing for compliments.

'You know how you look,' he said drily, refusing to rise to the bait. 'Beautiful—as ever. Are you ready?'

She nodded. 'You look pretty good yourself, you know,' she told him, feasting her eyes. His dinner suit was beautifully cut, the fine black wool in stark contrast to the blinding white shirt with its crisp pintucks down the front, and the bow-tie looked real.

He saw the direction of her eyes and patted it to check it. 'Is it all right?' he asked, and she nodded.

'It's fine.'

'Shall we go, then? Sue's settled in the sitting room with the television, and the children are all sorted.'

Sue Faulkner, the receptionist from the surgery, was babysitting for him, as she had done previously. Chrissie, of course, had been adamant that they didn't need a babysitter, but Xavier refused to leave her in sole charge of Nick, and anyway Fran knew he was reluctant to leave them alone in the house in case anything should happen and she was unable to help herself.

So Sue was there, and they were free to go.

They parked at the surgery, only a short walk along the quay to the gallery, and when they arrived she was glad that she'd bought her new dress.

It was a very classy do, as she might have imagined, and anyone of any significance in the town seemed to be there.

There were some strange metal figures in the middle of the room which Fran thought were a little gaunt and tortured, but some of the pictures really appealed to her. They reminded her oddly of the pictures in Josh's hall, and she wondered if they were by the same artist.

They had a haunting quality that really appealed to her, and she would happily have taken any one of them home.

And then she turned the corner and saw it, and her breath caught in her throat.

'Oh,' she breathed, and Xavier shot her a keen look, then followed the direction of her eyes.

'Do you like it?' he asked her, and she nodded slowly.

'I had a dream,' she said. 'I was walking by the river, and the mist was curling over the water, and it looked just like that. And then, the other night when I went to Josh's, it was misty just the same. It was so beautiful.'

She laughed self-consciously, wondering if she sounded stupid, but Xavier was studying her thoughtfully and he wasn't laughing.

'Do you regret not taking his job?' he asked her softly, and she looked at him in amazement. Was he jealous?

'No, I don't regret it,' she told him. 'How could I, when I'm with you?'

His eyes softened and he smiled and bent forward and brushed his lips over her cheek.

'Thank you.'

Just then, Josh came up to them, looking much better than he had three days before, although rather tired.

'I'm glad you could both make it,' he said with a smile. 'Help yourselves to wine, and feel free to buy anything you like,' he added, his eyes twinkling. 'Have you got a catalogue?'

They hadn't, so he hijacked one from a circulating minion and gave it to them, then, excusing himself, he moved on to talk to some other guests, leaving them to look around the rest of the exhibition.

There were some wonderful things, more of the pictures by a young woman called Annie who had done the one Fran liked, and some others by a thin, tortured young man called Joe. They were interesting, but none of them appealed to Fran in the way that the picture of the mist on the river did, and Fran found herself drawn to it again and again.

Xavier was commandeered by one of his patients, and while he was busy she stood and looked longingly at it.

'You really love it, don't you?'

She turned and looked up at Josh and gave him a wry smile.

'I do, but it isn't going to do me any good. I simply can't afford it. Well, not if I'm going to be able to buy anything else for the next six months, let's put it like that!'

Josh returned her smile. 'Maybe you should just buy it and worry about paying for it later. There are some things that we have to be sensible about, and others where perhaps we need to be a little rash. I'm a great believer in grabbing opportunities, because second chances don't come very often.'

He was very persuasive, but Fran refused to be talked into it. It was all very well for him to talk about being rash, but they were hardly in the same financial position.

'I'll think about it,' Fran promised him.

'You could have a second chance with me,' Josh said softly, 'but I rather think you've already made your choice.' He looked past her to where Xavier was standing, talking to his patient, and she felt soft colour flood her cheeks.

'Is it so obvious?' she asked him, and he gave a gentle smile.

'Probably not to everybody, but I should think all the single men in this room are well aware, and probably half the married ones. You may not know this, but there's a hands-off notice posted on your back.'

She almost turned to look for it, and then saw the twinkling in his eyes. She swallowed hard and looked away, and he chuckled softly.

'Don't worry about it. You just go for it, Fran. He's a good guy, if my mother's to be believed, and you look happy. I'm glad for you.'

He leant forward and kissed her cheek, then nodded at Xavier and walked off, leaning heavily on his crutch. Moments later Xavier was back at her side.

'What was that about?' he asked, watching Josh's retreat curiously.

'Oh, he was just trying to persuade me to buy the picture,' Fran said lightly, reluctant to tell him everything. To be honest, she didn't even know how to. What could she say? Josh says you're warning all the men off? Hardly—but it did give her a warm glow inside.

They left the exhibition shortly after that, and Xavier took her to a little restaurant in town for dinner and spoiled her. As they pulled up outside the house two hours later, Xavier cut the engine and turned to her, grazing her jaw with his knuckles.

'I wish tonight didn't have to end here,' he said softly.

She could have argued, but she didn't, because he was right, of course. Instead, she turned her head and pressed her lips to the palm of his hand, and his breath caught and he drew her to him in the darkness.

'They'll see,' she murmured, but he shook his head.

'No. The outside lights haven't come on yet.'

His lips found hers unerringly, and she stopped protesting and gave herself up to his kiss. All too soon he drew away, straightening up with a sigh and putting his hands back on the steering-wheel.

'You go on in, I'm going to put the car in the garage,' he said, and she went inside and spoke to Sue, who was idly watching something not very gripping on television.

'The kids have been fine,' she told Fran. 'I haven't heard a peep out of them, which is probably bad news, but when I went up a little while ago Chrissie was reading and Nick was asleep.'

She folded the paper that was lying on her lap, put it back on the coffee-table and gathered her things together. 'Did you have a good time?' she asked, and Fran smiled and nodded.

'Lovely, thank you. The exhibition was wonderful.'

'And the dinner?'

Fran nodded again. 'Very nice.'

'It's good to see him getting out again,' Sue said quietly. 'He's been almost reclusive—devoted himself entirely to the children and hardly done anything for himself since Sara died. It's high time he went out and enjoyed himself for a change, and I'm really pleased he's found you. I hope you're happy together.'

Fran opened her mouth to contradict Sue, then shut it. There was no point in lying to another woman, especially one who saw both of them so much. Instead, she said nothing, and seconds later Xavier came in and she excused herself.

She went into the kitchen and put the kettle on, and a few moments later she heard the front door close and then the firm, even tread of his footsteps crossing the hall.

'Coffee?' she said brightly, but he just came up behind her and put his arms round her and rested his head on her shoulder.

'That would be lovely. We can take it to the study. I'm going up to see the kids and change into something more relaxed. I'll be back in a minute.'

He pressed his lips to the soft skin below her ear, sending a shiver down her spine, and then with a sigh he pulled away and went upstairs.

Chrissie's light was still on, and he put his head

round the door and waggled his fingers at her. 'OK?' he asked, and she nodded.

'It's late. You need to go to sleep now,' he told her, and obediently she put her book down and turned out the light.

He was under no illusions. He went into the room, kissed her goodnight and put the book out of reach. 'Enough,' he said quietly. 'You'll be exhausted. I'll see you in the morning. Love you. Sleep well.'

He pulled the door to, but he didn't close it. She couldn't call him, and when she needed help she rang a little hand bell. It was always enough to wake him—parental instinct, probably, he thought. Sometimes he thought he would sleep through anything he was so tired, but her little bell would register.

That, and Fran's cries when she had a nightmare. Was he as attuned to her? How thought-provoking.

He went into his bedroom to change out of his suit, and as he was putting his cuff-links away, he picked up the picture of Sara that sat on the dressing-table. Suddenly it seemed inappropriate to have it there, as if it was a part of his life that he had left behind, and with a decisive snap he folded the stand and put the picture into the drawer with the cuff-links.

He was ready to move on, he realised, and only Chrissie's deep psychological trauma was preventing it. If only he could find the key...

The following morning Fran lay in bed and pondered on Josh's words. She'd dreamed about the river again, and in a moment of rashness she decided to buy the picture. She couldn't afford it, not really, not without dipping into her meagre savings, but, like Josh had said, with some things there were no second chances.

She got up, showered and dressed and drove her little car into town. It seemed oddly small and very easy to park compared to the people carrier she drove when she was ferrying the children, but she felt a little vulnerable in it.

How strange. She'd always liked it before.

She parked at the surgery, as they had the night before, and almost ran down to the gallery. It was thronged with people who had come to witness the opening of a new local attraction, and Fran had to worm her way through the crowd to the office at the back.

'I'd like to reserve a picture,' she said to the woman in charge. Catherine, she thought her name was.

'Which one would that be?'

'It's one of Annie's—the one of the mist on the river.'

'Oh, that one—I'm sorry, it's been reserved.'

Fran's heart sank. 'Oh. Oh, I see. Are you sure? Could you check? It's number 13.'

'Yes. Yes, I'm quite sure, a gentleman phoned up and reserved it this morning, and he's paid for it by credit card, so I'm afraid there's no chance it'll become available. I'm so sorry. What about one of the others?'

But Fran didn't want one of the others, and now she was kicking herself.

'It doesn't matter—I couldn't afford it anyway,' she said quietly, and went home to her little flat and chastised herself for the rest of the morning because she'd been too slow.

Xavier had taken the children out somewhere, and so she called the dogs and went for a walk, out along the lane that was almost opposite and down towards Bromeswell over the fields.

They went as far as the railway and then came back. The dogs were disgustingly muddy but content, and Fran shut them up in the boot room until they'd dried off a bit then made herself a cup of coffee.

It was lunchtime really, but with nobody else there it seemed rather pointless eating. Then she found a note from Xavier, telling her that they'd gone out for the day and would be back at about four.

If she hadn't listened to Josh and gone down to the gallery, maybe they would have invited her to go with them and she wouldn't have been alone for the day. Frustrated and cross and still very disappointed about the picture, Fran turned out the kitchen cupboards and scrubbed them from end to end.

On Monday Xavier was off in the afternoon, so he picked the children up from school and took Chrissie to her physio. Nick was sitting in the car, playing with his GameBoy, and Xavier was in the waiting room, sitting by the window, keeping an eye on his son and waiting for Chrissie.

She came out, followed by the physio, who came up to him with a careful professional smile.

'Dr Giraud. How nice to see you. Perhaps as you're here, you'd like to review Chrissie's progress. Have you got a moment?'

Puzzled, he followed her into the treatment room and closed the door, leaving Chrissie outside.

The physio turned to him, her smile gone. 'Dr Giraud, I wanted to talk to you because I'm frankly puzzled.'

'She's not worse? You haven't found something?'

he asked, panic rising in his chest, but she shook her head.

'No, far from it. She's better—she's stronger, she's putting on muscle. If I didn't know better, I'd say she was exercising. Maybe she's doing it on her own, walking round her room or something when you aren't there, or just lifting her legs—I don't know. It's peculiar, but it's not just her leg muscles. Her back's stronger, too. I just wondered if you could shed any light on it.'

He shook his head. 'No. No, none at all. I'm delighted, but I have no idea why it is. Maybe her swimming? Perhaps she's using her legs more, maybe without realising it.'

'It's possible. Think about it and let me know. I'd be fascinated to know why.'

He nodded. 'Sure. Thank you. I'll see what I can come up with.'

He took the children home, meaning to speak to Fran about it, but there wasn't a chance to get her alone before supper, and then after supper she said she had a headache and went to bed.

He didn't want to ask Chrissie, though, so he decided to bide his time and think about it and watch for signs.

He tucked her up in bed later, moved her book out of reach and checked it next morning, but it was still there, which made him think she wasn't walking round the room—unless she was smart enough to put it back again, of course, which wouldn't surprise him.

He resolved to talk to Fran, but yet again there were no opportunities, and it was Wednesday before he had any time to himself.

He went home at lunchtime, but Fran had gone,

and he remembered that it was Chrissie's day for swimming. Frustrated yet again, he made himself some lunch, walked the dogs and then got into the car and went out into the country for a drive.

It was a lovely day, clear and bright and sunny, and he found himself going past the stables where Chrissie used to ride. He glanced across at the stable yard and frowned, slowing the car and coming to a stop.

That looked like his people carrier, he thought, and, turning onto the track, he drove slowly towards the gate until he could see the registration plate.

It was his car—but what on earth was it doing here?

He opened the gate, drove through it and parked beside the people carrier, puzzled. Had Fran brought Chrissie to see the ponies?

And then he saw Chrissie's wheelchair parked by the end of the barn, and realisation dawned. She was riding. That was why her legs were stronger, why the physio couldn't understand the improvement.

Fran had brought her here—even though they'd discussed it and he'd said no—and had allowed her to ride.

Rage boiled up in him and, striding up the track to the sand school, he turned the corner and paused beside the entrance, rooted to the spot.

Chrissie was riding round on an old grey pony—unless he was mistaken, the one she used to ride before—trotting down the centre of the school over a series of poles, rising and falling naturally with the rhythm of the pony. Riding properly, as if there were nothing wrong with her.

She reached the end of the school and turned towards him, and her face lit up. She called him over, waving her arms frantically, and when he drew level with her, she bent down and hugged him.

'Well done,' he said, his voice almost unrecognisable. 'Well done.'

She beamed and flung her arms around the pony's neck, hugging her tight, and then sat up again, turning the pony towards a little jump. With a little squeeze of her legs she urged the pony forward into a trot, and popped the poles with ease.

And then she laughed, and his breath jammed in his chest and he had to blink hard to clear his eyes. She was better—much better, almost right again—and Fran hadn't condescended to tell him.

The rage rose up in him again, drowning out reason, and he turned to her, his voice deathly quiet.

'How dare you do this without consulting me?' he said. 'I want you to take her home, and then you and I are going to have a long talk, and if you're very lucky, I won't be taking legal action against you.'

He turned his back on her and went over to Chrissie.

'Time to go home,' he said, and something in his face must have communicated itself to her because the joy died in her eyes and she looked down and nodded.

'Good.'

He turned and walked away, forcing himself to drive home slowly and not break the speed limit. What he felt like doing was ramming his fist through something—something hard, like an oak tree or a wall.

He went straight past the house to the woodshed,

picked up the axe and slammed it through an old log, sending the pieces flying. Good. A few hundred more of them and he might have his anger under control.

And then he'd deal with Fran.

# CHAPTER TEN

FRAN felt sick. She'd never seen Xavier so angry, and she had a feeling that it was only the tip of the iceberg.

Louise, instantly picking up on the atmosphere, had caught Misty's reins and was leading her out of the sand school, with a subdued and very chastened Chrissie on board.

Fran caught up with them, putting her hand on Chrissie's leg.

'Don't worry, Chrissie, I'll deal with him,' she said reassuringly, but it was empty reassurance. She wasn't sure she could deal with him, or that there was any way that she could talk her way out of this.

Louise helped Chrissie into the wheelchair while Fran opened the car and pulled down the ramp, then she was clipped in and they were on their way home. Fran glanced at her watch. She had to collect Nick in ten minutes, and she didn't know if Xavier was doing it or not, but she didn't want to leave Nick standing there outside the school in case Xavier wasn't.

'I'm going to get Nick,' she told Chrissie, meeting her eyes in the rear-view mirror.

Chrissie nodded, her eyes wide with dread, but Fran couldn't reassure her. Xavier was going to be furious with both of them, and there was no way around it.

Nick, of course, took one look at their faces and went white.

158

'What is it?' he asked in a still, quiet voice Chrissie had never heard him use. 'Is it Dad?'

'He's all right,' Fran hastened to assure him, suddenly realising the source of his fear. 'Nothing's happened to him. He's cross with me, that's all. It's all right, Nick, it's nothing to do with you—you're not in trouble.'

Unlike me, she thought as she drove the short distance to the house and pulled up outside.

Xavier's car was on the drive, abandoned in a slew of gravel, and she closed her eyes and counted to ten before getting Chrissie out and heading for the door, a worried-looking Nick trailing in their wake.

As they reached the door it swung open, and Xavier stood there, his face etched with cold fury.

'Chrissie, go to your room. I'll talk to you later. Fran, my study—now.'

Chrissie hesitated, but Fran put a hand on her shoulder and squeezed it gently. 'It's all right, Chrissie. You go on up, I'll talk to your father,' she said soothingly.

After another quick glance at him, Chrissie wheeled her chair towards the stairs, and Fran drew in a steadying breath and walked towards Xavier. He was standing in the study, holding the door open, and the moment she was through it, it clicked shut behind her.

'Xavier, I can explain,' she began, but he cut her off.

'I doubt it,' he said, his voice deathly quiet. 'Without my knowledge or consent, you took my daughter riding, after we'd already discussed it and I'd said no. As far as I can see, there is nothing to explain.'

'You didn't say no—and we didn't discuss it. Not riding, not exactly. We discussed the RDA—'

'This is semantics! I said no, Fran, and you deliberately went behind my back and defied me! You and Chrissie planned this between you—'

'No! No, that's not how it happened. Louise is a friend of mine—I went to see her, and told her where I was working. She asked about Chrissie. I took her down there to see the pony, to see if I could get a reaction out of her. Which I did. She asked if she could ride her, and I said she had to tell you.'

'And she didn't, so you had no business taking her.'

'She made me promise. She said there was no point in telling you until she was sure she could do it, because she didn't want to disappoint you. Then she said she wanted to wait until she was good enough. If she managed to go over that fence today, she was going to tell you. She promised, and I told her I wasn't taking her again unless she did.'

'And if she'd fallen off and hurt herself? For God's sake, Fran, she's been through enough!' he yelled, finally losing control. 'Can't you understand? A blow to the head, a twist to the spine—whatever was wrong with her could have been stirred up again—'

'But there's nothing wrong with her—you told me that! You said she was locked inside and you couldn't find the key—well, I found it, Xavier, and I wanted to tell you. I've wanted so much to tell you, and we've argued about it over and over again, but she wanted to surprise you—'

'Well, she certainly did that, and so did you. I thought I could trust you, Fran. I thought we had a relationship based on honesty and trust, and you betrayed my trust.'

'Well, better yours than your daughter's,' she yelled back at him. 'What was I supposed to do? She was happy, Xavier—she laughed, for goodness' sake! Her legs were getting stronger, her behaviour had improved—you said yourself she was a different girl. I didn't dare do anything that might damage that, anything that could hinder her progress or set her back to square one. How could I tell you? And, anyway, I'd given her my word.'

'You should never have done that,' he said coldly. 'You should have refused, right at the beginning.'

'What, and thrown away the key? I did it for you as much as Chrissie, to free you from the worry and the guilt that's plagued you since the accident, so you could move on and be happy again.'

'With you.'

'If that was what you chose. I hoped it would be. You seemed to be happy with me—at least in bed.'

He gave a short, humourless laugh and his eyes, those lovely eyes that she'd thought the kindest eyes she'd ever seen, slashed through her like knives. So did his next words.

'Just sex, Fran. That's all it was. And you thought we had a future together? I don't think so. I don't want you in my life, Fran. I can't trust you, and without trust there's nothing.'

'Xavier, you told me to use my judgement with the children. You gave me responsibility, handed it over. I did nothing I thought you wouldn't do under the circumstances. Chrissie was riding the same pony she had before, in the same place, and if it was all right then, why not now? You'd sanctioned it then.'

'That was different. Sara took her. I never liked it, I always thought it was too dangerous.'

'You said you'd talked about buying her a pony.'

'Sara talked about it. I said no—as I said no about taking her riding.'

'No. No, you didn't. You said you'd taken her to the RDA, and it was awful because the kids there had head injuries, but she was in the wrong group. There are lots of different groups, for people with all kinds of problems, but you wouldn't let me tell you about it. Louise knows—she runs an RDA group from there, and she knew what she was doing. Chrissie was never in danger, Xavier, I wouldn't have done that to her, I swear.'

Her voice cracked, and she turned away, swallowing hard. Dammit, she wouldn't cry, she wouldn't! She had to fight this one out for Chrissie, and she wouldn't think about his words, not now, not yet.

*Just sex, Fran.*

She dragged in some air.

'You did do it to her—and without telling me. Don't you think I would have been interested in her progress? How do you think I felt when the physio told me on Monday that she was getting stronger? I didn't know why, and I wanted to ask you, but there hasn't been a moment. You went to bed early on Monday, with a headache. How convenient. Was that because you knew the physio would have spoken to me?'

She shook her head. 'No—and if you'd talked to me, I would have made you talk to Chrissie. I still wouldn't have told you myself.'

'You're just trying to put the blame on her, aren't you?' he said furiously, and the hatred in his eyes cut her to the quick. 'You're trying to blame all this on the child, and pretend you were just manipulated, when all the time you were doing this for your own ends. You just wanted me, and the house, and the kids, and you thought if Chrissie was better you could have that—I don't believe it!'

She stood there in silence, unable to reply, because in a way he was right, although not in the cold, calculating way he made it sound. Yes, she'd done it for herself, but for all of them really, to free them all from the terrible burden of Chrissie's incapacity, and now it had all gone wrong and heaven knows what harm it would do her.

'Fran, I want you out of here. You've got ten minutes to pack your things, and I want you gone, and I never want to see you again.'

'Daddy, no!'

They turned, startled to see Chrissie standing in the doorway, holding onto the knob for dear life, tears streaming down her face.

'No!' she croaked. 'Don't send her away. It's my fault. It's always my fault. It's always because of something I do. That's why Mummy died, and now you're sending Fran away, and it's my fault again.'

'Darling, it's not your fault,' he said, crossing the room swiftly and catching her before she fell. He scooped her up in his arms and sat down on the chesterfield, cradling her against his chest.

'It's my fault,' she was sobbing, and he rocked her and smoothed the lank strands of hair from her damp forehead and made her look at him.

'No, it isn't. It's my fault. I should have taken more notice of what you were doing, asked you.'

'I wouldn't have told you, and that was wrong, and

now Fran's got to go, just like Mummy, because I was so stupid.'

'What are you talking about, Chrissie? What's this got to do with your mother?' he asked, and Fran pulled Nick into her arms and held him while they listened to her halting words.

'Nick and I were fighting—in the car. Mummy said, "Will you two stop that or there's going to be an accident," and then there was a car just there...'

'But the driver was dead,' Xavier said gently. 'Chrissie, it was nobody's fault. He'd died at the wheel—the car was out of control. It was just an accident, nothing else. It certainly wasn't your fault.'

'I didn't know he was dead. I thought he'd died, too—in the accident. Nobody told me...'

She broke off and started crying, great heaving sobs, and Fran turned Nick and ushered him out into the hall.

'Is she all right?' he asked tentatively, and Fran hugged him.

'Yes. Yes, I think she's fine. I think she's finally free of whatever it was that's kept her like this for so long. Guilt, I think. I don't know, but she's talking, and that's a huge start, don't you think?'

He nodded, and then looked up at her. 'Are you really going?' he asked, and she nodded.

'I'm afraid so,' she said quietly.

His eyes filled with tears, and he broke away from her and ran upstairs. She heard the door bang, then the sound of muffled sobs, and she closed her eyes and let the tears slip down her cheeks.

Just sex. That was all it had meant to Xavier, nothing more. Still, he'd never told her that he loved her, although he'd said other things about how much she meant to him, but mostly that had been about sharing responsibility and nothing to do with their personal relationship, the strength of the bond between them.

And now that bond was severed.

Fran brushed away the tears and went upstairs to her flat, packing her few meagre possessions into her case. Some of her things that she'd brought from London were still in bags and boxes in the bottom of her wardrobe, and she pulled them out and piled them on the bed.

So little to show for her twenty-seven years. She had nowhere to go, nothing to do with the rest of her life. It was a good job she hadn't bought the picture, she thought. Where could she have put it?

There was a knock on the door, and she turned to find Xavier standing there, his face ravaged with tears.

'Chrissie wants you to stay,' he said, his accent stronger than ever.

'Is she all right?'

'I think so. It was the accident—nobody talked to her about it. She was so distressed every time it was mentioned that we avoided it, so she never knew the truth. I've left her looking at the press cuttings in my study. I said I'd come and talk to you—ask you to stay.'

'And what about you?' she asked. 'Do you want me to stay?'

'I don't know what I want,' he said raggedly. 'I just know I can't trust you, and I find that impossible to deal with.'

'Then there's no question about it. I'll have to go. If you don't trust me, I can't do my job with the children, and I can't stay just for Chrissie.'

'She says she won't talk and she won't walk unless you stay. She says that's why she was in the wheelchair and didn't talk after her mother died—so she couldn't cause any more disasters—and if you go, she'll do it again.'

Fran closed her eyes. She couldn't stay—not like this, with Xavier hating her. And yet how could she leave?

'All right—but only for a while, just until she's settled. Until Christmas, maybe.'

'That's only two weeks.'

She looked up and met his eyes. 'Xavier, I can't—'

She broke off, tears welling up in her eyes again, and with an exasperated sigh she dashed them aside and turned away, wrapping her arms around her waist and hanging on for dear life.

'I can't stay any longer. I never meant this to happen. I was only trying to help Chrissie, to find the key—I didn't want to keep you in the dark, but she insisted. If you only knew how much I've hated having secrets from you—'

'Stop it, Fran. It's too late. You should have thought of that before. So, what do I tell Chrissie? Will you stay, for her?'

'But not for you.'

'No. Not for me. Not for us. There is no us any more, Fran. Not now.'

Could she do it? Was she strong enough?

She had to be, otherwise Chrissie would be back in the wheelchair and condemned to silence again, and she couldn't do that to her.

Her shoulders drooped. 'All right. Tell her I'll stay for a while—if you think you can trust me to look after them without damaging them.'

'I have no choice,' he said flatly.

The door clicked shut and Fran sank down on the edge of the bed in the midst of her possessions and stared sightlessly out of the window. She couldn't even escape, couldn't run away and hide from her pain. She had to stay here, trapped, and pretend she was all right, for the children's sake.

She drew in a shuddering breath and let it out again, then stood up and went into her bathroom. Her face was awful, red and blotchy and tear-stained, but she guessed she wasn't alone. She washed it in cold water, patted it dry and went down to the kitchen to start the supper.

There was no one there, and so she was able to work without distraction, but all that meant was going through the events of the past few weeks and hours over and over again in her mind, until she thought she'd go crazy.

There wasn't anything else she could have done, she thought, without betraying Chrissie's confidence. If she'd told Xavier, and he'd refused to let Chrissie go again, then her progress, so tentative, so fragile, would have been halted. She couldn't have risked that, even at the risk of her own personal happiness.

What could that matter compared to the life of a child?

Fran shook her head slowly and forced herself to concentrate on cooking. She was making a cheese and potato and onion gratin, with sausages for Xavier and Nick from the butcher in a nearby village, but after she'd put it in the oven she realised she'd left out the onion.

She pulled it back out and burned herself on the oven rack, and it was the last straw. Dropping the pan on the floor, she ran out of the door and down the garden, finally sinking to the ground at the base of a tree.

She leant against the trunk, tears streaming down her face, and sobbed her heart out.

Xavier walked into the kitchen to a scene of devastation. There was an oven dish on the floor, the remains of the contents spread liberally about on the tiles, and the dogs were busy clearing up the last few scraps of what looked like raw potato.

There was no sign of Fran, but the back door was open and as he went out into the garden and stood still, he could hear her sobbing.

The sound tore at him, but he hardened his heart. She'd brought it on herself, and he was adamant. Without trust, they had nothing. It was all based on lies.

He went back into the kitchen, picked up the oven pan and put it in the dishwasher, wiped the last trace of cheese sauce off the floor and chased the dogs out into the garden. They'd find her and bring her back, and in the meantime, he needed to find something for supper.

Not that he was hungry, he didn't suppose any of them were, but they needed the routine to ground them.

He opened the freezer and stared blankly at the contents, but all he could see was Fran's face streaked with tears, and his vision blurred again.

'Damn,' he muttered, slamming the lid of the freezer. He went over to the phone on the dresser, called the local pizza place and placed an order. It would be delivered in half an hour, and that would solve that problem, if not the others.

Nothing would solve the others, he thought dispiritedly. He felt numb inside, torn in two. Part of him was hugely relieved about Chrissie and kicking himself for not discussing the accident with her earlier; the other part—well, he didn't want to think about the other part. It hurt too much, and he couldn't deal with it now.

Behind him, he heard the back door close and the sound of footsteps on the back stairs, and he shut his eyes and dragged in an agonised breath. How could she have betrayed his trust like that?

Better yours than your daughter's, she'd said, but she could have told him.

And then what? He would have stopped Chrissie riding.

Would he? He didn't know—and if he didn't, then surely Fran wouldn't have been sure.

Even so, she should have told him.

And risk it? Chrissie had trusted her.

And he'd trusted Fran.

He swore, softly and succinctly and in French, and turned to find Chrissie there in her wheelchair. 'Where's Fran?' she asked, her voice still very shaky.

'In her room.'

'Is she really staying?'

'I think so. I've ordered pizza—'

'I want to talk to her. I'll go up.'

She turned her wheelchair and scooted over to the stairs, then climbed unsteadily into the stair lift and went up. He watched her until she was out of sight, then sat down with a sigh. He needed to speak to Nick, but he was so raw at the moment he couldn't talk to anyone. He'd go up in a minute.

# CHAPTER ELEVEN

'FRAN?'

She straightened up from the bottom of the wardrobe and went to the communicating door. Chrissie was there, in her wheelchair, and her face was streaked with tears.

'Can I talk to you?'

'Chrissie, of course! Come in.'

Fran pushed her into the sitting room, then sat down beside her, taking her hands. 'Are you all right?'

Chrissie nodded dumbly. 'I think so. Are you really staying? Daddy said you were.'

'Yes,' she said. 'Yes, I'm staying. For a while, at least.'

Chrissie searched her face. 'A while?' she said cautiously. 'What about you and Daddy?'

'What about us?' Fran said, trying not to sound as devastated as she felt. 'We'll just go on as before, Chrissie. We're colleagues at work, and here I'm his housekeeper—his employee.'

'But—I thought—you seemed closer than that. More—you know—like you were having an affair.'

And they thought they'd hidden it from the children!

'No, sweetheart,' she lied. 'I just work here.'

'Then what did he mean about just sex?'

Fran closed her eyes. She couldn't get out of this one, clearly.

'Chrissie, don't worry about it,' she said quietly. 'That's nothing to do with this. It doesn't change anything.'

'Do you love him?' Chrissie asked her, cutting to the chase, and Fran's throat closed up.

'Yes,' she said softly. 'Yes, I love him, but he doesn't love me.'

'No, he hates you, and it's my fault. I tried to tell him it was my fault, but he wouldn't listen. I said I wouldn't let you tell him about the riding, that I made you keep it secret, but he just said it was wrong of you and I should have told him, and I said you'd told me that…'

She broke off, tears streaming down her face, and Fran reached over and hugged her.

'Chrissie, listen to me,' she said urgently. 'It isn't your fault. None of this is your fault. I should have told your father, or insisted that you did. I should have made you, instead of allowing you to dictate it. He needed to know, and we were both mistaken in keeping it from him, but you're only thirteen. I'm an adult, and I should have known better. And if our relationship isn't strong enough to weather this storm, well, then, it isn't, and it would have ended anyway. So, you see, it really doesn't matter. Nothing matters as much as you, sweetheart. Now, don't cry, please, or you'll start me off again and we'll both drown.'

Chrissie gave a tiny strangled laugh and sat up, sniffing and scrubbing her cheeks with her hands. Fran gave her a tissue, took one for herself and they mopped up together, sharing a watery smile.

'No more tears,' Fran made her promise. 'It's suppertime. I need to find something to cook us—I dropped the potato pie on the floor.'

'The dogs ate it. Daddy's ordered pizza.'

Fran struggled for a smile. 'Well, that's good. You all like pizza. You go on down, and I'll be down in a minute. Is Nick all right?'

'I don't know. He was crying, but he told me to go away.'

'I'll go and see him,' Fran promised, and followed Chrissie along the corridor and across the landing.

Chrissie went downstairs, and Fran continued on to Nick's room, knocking on the door.

'Go away,' he said, his voice muffled, but there was no way she was leaving him alone like this.

'Nick, it's Fran. Let me in.'

He unlocked the door and threw himself back onto the bed face down. She sat beside him and put a hand on his back, rubbing it soothingly.

'Nick, it's OK. I'm not going—at least not for a while.'

He lifted his head and went still. 'You're not?'

'No.'

He turned over and looked up at her, and his young face was filled with hope and confusion. She envied him. She only felt confusion.

'It's all right,' she said, and gathered him into her arms and hugged him.

He rested against her for a moment, then wriggled away, much too grown-up to endure a cuddle. 'So what's for supper?' he asked, and she suppressed a smile.

'Pizza. Your father's ordered it.'

'Are you coming down?'

She wasn't, but he was looking at her expectantly, and she didn't have the heart to turn him down.

'OK,' she said, but as they went downstairs she was dreading it.

She needn't have bothered. Xavier was back in control of his feelings and, apart from a distinct chill in the air as far as Fran was concerned, he was no different to normal.

Play-acting, Fran thought, and somehow she got through the meal without disgracing herself. They were all subdued, though, and Fran thought how sad it was when they should have been so happy for Chrissie.

Perhaps Xavier thought so, too, because at the end of the meal he raised his glass of water to Chrissie and gave her a strained smile.

'Welcome back, Chrissie,' he said softly, but she just burst into tears and wheeled herself away.

Fran started to stand up and follow her, but Xavier gave her a look that would have splintered diamonds and went after her himself. Fran sank back into her chair and wondered how on earth she was going to get through these next few weeks.

Xavier strode into the surgery the following morning and looked straight through Sue.

'Hold my first patients, and get Fran to come and see me when she arrives,' he told her. Picking up his notes, he went through into his consulting room without another word, leaving Sue open-mouthed.

Damn. He'd have to apologise to her later, but he was raw, so tight with emotion he could hardly function. He hadn't slept at all, and in the night he'd heard Fran crying.

He'd hardened himself to the sound, pulling the

quilt up round his ears to block it out, telling himself it was her own fault and she'd brought it on herself.

That didn't stop it hurting, though, and he ached for what they'd lost. A clean break would have been so much easier for all of them, but Chrissie was adamant, and what Chrissie wanted, at the moment, Chrissie got. She was too fragile to mess with, and he didn't dare risk this new breakthrough.

The first thing he did was phone the head of the school and tell him briefly what had happened. 'I don't want anyone to say anything, but you need to know that she's started speaking again. Can you warn her teachers and maybe her classmates? Her closest friends, anyway. I think they should know, even though she may decide not to talk just yet. It's been very emotional, as you can imagine.'

'Leave it with me,' the head said. 'We'll handle it very carefully. Who are her best friends?'

He gave him the names of three girls, and then there was a tap on the door and Fran came in, her face guarded. He ended his call and put the phone down, then glanced up at her.

'You wanted to see me,' she said, not looking at him.

That made it easier.

'Yes. About our relationship in the house. I think it would be easier if we didn't all eat together. I'll eat with the children, of course, and you're welcome to share our food, but I'd be grateful if you'd take yours upstairs. I think it would make it easier for all of us. And I'll get their breakfasts and make their lunches, and you can take over when I go to work. All right?'

'Fine. Anything else?'

'No.'

'Right. I'll get on, then,' she said, and left the room.

He closed his eyes and took a few seconds to compose himself, then called his first patient.

Well, it was certainly easier like this, Fran thought. She didn't see Xavier at work except in passing, and she didn't see him at home if she could possibly avoid it.

Chrissie was making steady progress, and she'd started talking at school as well as at home. It had taken a couple of days, but now she'd started she couldn't seem to stop and she was constantly on the phone to her friends. She was still using her wheelchair, but her legs were growing stronger every day.

There was no more riding, though, and none of them raised the subject.

Christmas was drawing closer by the minute, and Fran knew Xavier and the children were going to France, leaving on Christmas Day and coming back on New Year's Day. He'd arranged a locum months ago, and the dogs were booked into kennels, and Fran had planned to go to her parents in Devon for a few days.

She hadn't really wanted to go but now, suddenly, she couldn't wait to get away. The children broke up from school and, as agreed, Angie covered her work at the surgery and she stayed at home with the children for the two days before Christmas.

She bought them presents and gave them to them on Christmas Eve, just before she set off in the car to drive to her parents'.

'I wish you could come with us to France,' Chrissie said sadly as she said goodbye.

'You'll be so busy you won't even notice I'm not there,' Fran said bracingly, hugging them both. 'You be good, now, and don't wear your grandparents out. Take care.'

She kissed them, Chrissie on the cheek, Nick on the top of his head because that was all he would offer, and even that was a concession.

Xavier was standing unsmiling in the doorway, and for a moment they just looked at each other, then she turned away, slid behind the wheel and set off.

Home, at last. Xavier turned onto the drive and pulled up with a sigh of relief outside the beautiful little chateau that had been in the family for generations.

His mother came out, tall and elegant and looking far younger than her sixty years, and greeted the children with delight. She made a great fuss of Chrissie, crying and laughing, and hugged Nick hard and told him there were puppies in the barn.

She sent the children off to see them, then she looked up at Xavier and tutted gently, then drew him into her arms.

'What is it?' she asked him in French. 'You look awful.'

'Nothing, *Maman*. I'm just tired. It's a long story, I'll tell you later.'

'Xavier!'

He escaped his mother's embrace and hugged his father, standing back to look at him. 'You look well,' he said, forcing a smile, but his father wasn't fooled.

'More than can be said for you,' he retorted. 'What is it?'

He sighed. He might have known he couldn't hide his pain from them.

'Nothing. Please, just leave it.'

'Come inside. We'll have a glass of wine and talk about it.'

'I'd rather have a brandy.'

'No doubt, but drinking yourself into a stupor won't change whatever it is that's eating at you.'

They weren't going to let it go, he realised, so he gave in, accepted a glass of wine from his father and told them the edited highlights.

'Were you having an affair?'

He looked away. 'I don't think that's relevant, *Maman*.'

'So you were,' his mother said, unmoved. 'Is it the first?'

'Why?'

'Because of course you're hurting, if it is. It stands to reason.'

'*Maman*, my private life isn't, and never has been, any of your business,' he said gruffly.

'No, but your happiness is, and your children's happiness. Were you going to marry her?'

'No—of course not! It was just an affair. She knew that and so did I. I can't get involved with someone now, the children need me.'

'That's just an excuse,' his father said. 'Your children look fine to me—and, if anything, they need a mother. Besides, I thought it was because of this Fran that Chrissie started walking and talking again? Didn't you say that?'

He hadn't, not in so many words, but of course it was.

'She betrayed my trust.'

'She did exactly what you would have done under the circumstances. What is wrong with you, Xavier?

Are you jealous because she was the one to find the cure?'

He looked at his mother in astonishment. 'Of course not!'

'Then why get on your high horse? So she didn't tell you. So what? She had to choose between betraying one or the other of you. Better you than your traumatised thirteen-year-old daughter,' his mother said, echoing Fran's words almost exactly.

Of course, that was what you got for having a psychologist for a mother and a surgeon for a father. Cut-and-dried common sense.

'I don't think it's up to you to tell me how to conduct my life,' he said, getting to his feet. 'If you'll excuse me, I'm going to find the children and then we'll unpack.'

'The children are fine. Xavier, sit down and stop being defensive. Have another glass of wine and relax.'

His father topped up his glass and then sat down again, raising an expectant eyebrow. Xavier sat, giving up the unequal struggle and succumbing to their concern.

'I'm sorry,' he said a little gruffly. 'I'm just raw inside—I don't want to talk about it any more.'

'Of course not. We'll talk about something else. Are you hungry? Can I get you something, or shall we wait until dinner?'

He missed Fran. It was ridiculous how much he missed her, but his father's words kept echoing in his head. Had he overreacted because he was jealous that Fran, and not he, had found the cure? He didn't think so but, leaving that aside, had she done anything that he wouldn't have done in her shoes?

Probably not. And now here he was in France, miles from her, when he should have been there, sorting things out with her.

If they could be sorted.

And anyway, she was in Devon until the weekend, so he forced himself to join in the jollity. His brother and his wife were there with their three children, and a cousin dropped in, and everybody but him was having a great time.

He should have been. After all the misery of the past few years, he should have been over the moon because he'd got his daughter back, but all he could think about was Fran, and his heart was aching.

And then on Friday morning, less than forty-eight hours after they'd arrived, he had a phone call from Stuart, the senior partner, to say that the locum was sick with flu and they were stretched to the limit, and was there any possibility that he could come back or should he try and get another locum?

'I'll come home,' he said decisively. 'The kids will be fine here. I can work over the weekend and come back to fetch them on Tuesday evening. It's no problem.'

And he could see Fran when she got back.

He drove to Calais, by a miracle getting a slot on the Eurostar train, and he was home in time to do the evening surgery.

Stuart was pleased to see him, and in many ways he was glad to be back and away from all the forced *joie de vivre* that was going on at home.

His last patient left and he drove home, to find a

message on the answering machine, telling him that the picture was ready for collection at the gallery.

Fran's picture, the one of the river that she had loved so much.

He phoned them, and they were still there, taking down the exhibition, so he drove to the gallery and collected it. It was wrapped in brown paper, and he didn't look at it. He couldn't bring himself to, after all that had happened.

He debated going to the pub for supper but in the end, too tired and crabby to want company, he drove home. He'd have a brandy, put his feet up and wallow in self-pity, he decided.

Either that or try and track down Fran by ringing directory enquiries and getting the number of all the Williamses in Devon.

Probably not. The brandy, then, he decided, and turned onto the drive, coming to an abrupt halt.

Fran's car was there, the boot open, and he saw her standing beside it. He pulled up beside her and got out, walking cautiously over to her.

'Hello, Fran,' he said, unsure how to start. 'I didn't realise you were coming back so soon.'

'I've come to get my things,' she said, and, glancing into the boot, he realised that she'd packed everything.

'You're going?' he said hoarsely.

'I think it's best, don't you?'

He shook his head, his carefully rehearsed speeches all flying out of the window.

'No. Fran, don't leave. I've been a fool. I overreacted, and I would have done the same as you in the circumstances. You did it for Chrissie, and it worked, and, whatever my feelings about being consulted, what you did was right in the end, and I was wrong. I would have stopped you from taking her, and that would have been a huge mistake.'

She closed the boot of her car and stood there, leaning on it, emotions chasing over her face one after the other.

'Xavier, what are you saying?' she said unsteadily.

He dragged in a much-needed breath, and met her eyes.

'I'm saying I was wrong. I'm saying forgive me, and stay with us.' He paused and took another breath, then let it out shakily. 'I'm saying I love you. I didn't realise. I was so wrapped up with Chrissie that I didn't know what you'd come to mean to me until it was too late. You're my rock, Fran, my anchor. I need you. We all do, but me especially.'

He looked down at the gravel, scuffing it with his foot.

'Marry me, Fran,' he said roughly. 'Stay with me forever. Give me back my life, like you've given Chrissie hers.' His voice dropped to a low murmur. 'Be my wife, and have children with me, and be a part of our future. Please.'

She closed her eyes, and a single tear slipped down her cheek.

'I thought I'd lost you,' she said brokenly. 'I thought I'd destroyed what we had.'

'No. It was me that did that. Fran, I'm so sorry.'

'Don't be sorry, just hold me,' she whispered, and he didn't hesitate. He gathered her into his arms and held her hard against his heart, and after a moment she lifted her head and looked up at him.

'I didn't think you'd be here. I was going to take

everything and just go, because I hate goodbyes. Where are the children?'

'In France, with my parents. My locum was sick so I had to come home. Well—I didn't have to. I could have got someone else, but it gave me a good excuse. I wanted to see you. I knew you were coming back this weekend, and I needed to talk to you.'

He remembered something and, releasing her, he went to his car.

'I've got something for you,' he said. 'It was meant to be your Christmas present, but maybe you could have it as a wedding present instead.' He opened the boot and took out the picture, and she stared at it hopefully.

'Is…that…?'

'The picture? Yes.'

'I went back for it the next day, and you must have just phoned them,' she told him. 'I was so upset.' She ran her fingers lovingly over the paper wrapping.

'I'm sorry. Maybe I should have told you, but I wanted it to be a surprise. Where shall we hang it?'

'Your study?'

'There's a space over the fireplace, or it can go in the hall. There's room.'

'I don't care. Wherever it goes, I'll love it.' She looked at him warily. 'Did you mean that? About a wedding present?'

He studied her face, so afraid to believe. Putting the picture down carefully, he drew her into his arms again.

'Yes,' he said emphatically. 'Yes, I meant it. Will you marry me?'

'Oh, Xavier…'

She threw herself into his arms, and when they

came up for air, he smiled down at her and touched the tip of her nose with his finger.

'I take it that was a yes?' he said softly, and she laughed.

'That was a yes.'


Xavier pulled up outside his parents' house on Tuesday afternoon, and the children came out to greet him.

Fran stayed in the car, suddenly smitten by nerves. It was one thing to be a favoured nanny-cum-housekeeper, it was quite another to take a mother's place.

Then Xavier said something to them and they saw her, and both of them started to run towards her.

She got out, reaching out for them and gathering them up in her arms, and then they were all laughing and crying and hugging each other.

'I missed you so much,' Chrissie said.

Nick added, 'Me, too. Fran, there are puppies.'

'Are there? I must see them.'

'I've been riding,' Chrissie said. 'I sat on one of Uncle Christian's racehorses, and it was brilliant! He said I was very good.'

'What, the horse said that?' Xavier teased, and she laughed at him and hugged him again.

Then Fran looked up at the grey-haired couple standing on the steps of the chateau with their arms around each other, beaming at her, and she let go of the children and went towards them with Xavier.

'*Maman*, *Papa*, I'd like you to meet Fran. We're getting married,' he added, looking down into her eyes, and she thought her heart would burst with happiness.

'Welcome to the family,' his father said, kissing her on the cheek, and his mother hugged her, and then they were in the kitchen and champagne corks were popping, and in the midst of it all Xavier turned to Fran and said, 'I love you.'

Tears welled up in her eyes, and she groped in her coat pocket for a tissue. Something else fell out, fluttering to the floor, and he picked it up and handed it to her.

She glanced at it, and smiled.

'What is it?'

'Nothing,' she said, tearing Josh's business card up and putting it in the bin. 'I don't need it any more. I only need you.'

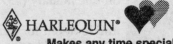

*For better, for worse...*
*these marriages were meant to last!*

They've already said "I do," but what happens
when their promise to love, honor and cherish
is put to the test?

Emotions run high as husbands and wives discover
how precious—and fragile—their wedding vows
are...but their love will keep them together—forever!

**Look out for the following in**

**MAYBE MARRIED by Leigh Michaels
(#3731) on-sale January**

**THE PRODIGAL WIFE by Susan Fox
(#3740) on-sale March**

And watch out for other bestselling authors appearing
in this popular miniseries throughout 2003.

*Available wherever Harlequin books are sold.*

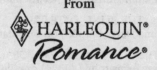

## MEN WHO TURN YOUR
## WHOLE WORLD UPSIDE DOWN!

Strong and silent...
Powerful and passionate...
Tough and tender...

Who can resist the rugged loners of the Outback?
As tough and untamed as the land they rule, they
burn as hot as the Australian sun once they meet
the women they've been waiting for.

# THE WEDDING CHALLENGE
by
Harlequin Romance® rising star

## *Jessica Hart*

on-sale February (#3736)

Feel the Outback heat throughout 2003,
with Harlequin Romance® authors:
**Margaret Way, Barbara Hannay and Darcy Maguire!**

*And don't miss these stories of seduction and passion by
Australian Harlequin Presents® authors:*

THE BLIND-DATE BRIDE
Emma Darcy (#2308) on-sale March

HIS CONVENIENT PROPOSAL
Lindsay Armstrong (#2324) on-sale May